ABOUT THIS BOOK

The sequel to *Awaken the Soul*, this novella continues the story of Breckin and Vivienne, whose hearts and souls are once again on the line.

Nearly dying, being stalked by a reaper, and finding her soulmate, all before Christmas, were not items on Vivienne Freeman's senior year bucket list. Now that Vivienne's survived December, Breckin Roberts decides they've had enough excitement for one year. As January rolls around, he is determined they will finish out their school year like normal teens. Except there's nothing normal about these two.

When Vivienne's supernatural abilities manifest, Breckin questions whether the changes are due to their soul bond, his healing her, or something more. They turn to Elias for answers, only to discover there's an entire history connecting their families they knew nothing about.

As the fallen descend on Havenwood Falls, Vivienne and Breckin are caught in a fight bigger than themselves. They must unravel the secrets and avenge the heart before any chance of redemption is lost forever.

HAVENWOOD FALLS HIGH BOOKS

Written in the Stars by Kallie Ross

Reawakened by Morgan Wylie

The Fall by Kristen Yard

Somewhere Within by Amy Hale

Awaken the Soul by Michele G. Miller

Bound by Shadows by Cameo Renae

Fata Morgana by E.J. Fechenda

Forever Emeline by Katie M. John

Reclamation by AnnaLisa Grant

Avenoir by Daniele Lanzarotta

Avenge the Heart by Michele G. Miller

Curse the Night by R.K. Ryals

Blood & Iron by Amy Hale

Shadows & Spells by Cameo Renae

Falling Deep by J.L. Weil

Saving Infiniti by Rose Garcia

Willful by Liz Ferry

Cast in Moonlight by Ali Winters

Promise the Moon by Kallie Ross

Blurred Lines by Daniele Lanzarotta

Ascending Darkness by J.L. Weil

Finding Infiniti by Rose Garcia

Unicorn's Lament by Megan Linski

Paper Bird by Amy Richie

Predestined by Valia Lind

Rediscovered by Morgan Wylie

Ashes of Fate by Apryl Baker

Stay up to date at www.HavenwoodFalls.com

ALSO BY MICHELE G. MILLER

From The Wreckage Series - Coming of Age Drama

From The Wreckage

Out of Ruins

All That Remains

West: A POV Novel

After the Fall - Austin's story (New Adult)

Into the Fire - Dani's story

The Prophecy of Tyalbrook Trilogy - YA Fantasy Romance

Never Let You Fall

Never Let You Go

Never Without You (Coming 2018)

Individual titles

Last Call (New Adult Romance)

Awaken the Soul, A Havenwood Falls High novella (YA Fantasy)

Avenge the Heart, A Havenwood Falls High novella (YA Fantasy)

CO-WRITTEN WITH MINDY HAYES

Paper Planes Series - Sweet Contemporary Romances

Paper Planes and Other Things We Lost (YA)

Subway Stops and the Places We Meet (Adult)

Chasing Cars and the Lessons We Learned (NA)

The Backroads Duet – Sweet Contemporary Romances

Love in C Minor

Loss in A Major (Coming July 27, 2018)

Nothing Compares 2 U, a 10 Things I Love About You novella

Visit Michele's website for updates

http://www.michelegmillerbooks.com/

AVENGE THE HEART

A HAVENWOOD FALLS HIGH NOVELLA

MICHELE G. MILLER

For Mindy

IT HAS BEGUN

VIVIENNE

"*Why* are you so glowy?" Zara asks in her faux British accent as she drops her ice skates on the wooden floor and lowers herself into the vacant seat across from me at Coffee Haven.

"Well, hello to you, too."

"Oh my gosh! You're pregnant!"

I choke. Thank God I hadn't taken a drink of my coffee. "What?"

"You are radiant, Viv. Like ridiculously so."

Careful not to crush the paper cup in my hand, I lean across the table and look my best friend in the eyes. "So, I'm pregnant?"

"Well, you are with Breckin . . ."

"And?" I bite the inside of my cheek.

"He's hot, and Breckin Roberts. And you're together twenty-four seven."

"My boyfriend is hot, so logically speaking, I'm pregnant." I return to my casual position. "It's happened—you've finally gone mad."

Zara's dark eyes study me intently. How much could I have changed since last night? I kick her shin. "Stop dissecting me. I'm not pregnant."

Her freshly manicured red nail taps her chin. "Are you positive?"

"Yes, I'm positive," I hiss. "You have to have sex to get pregnant.

1

I'm not having sex, Z. Plus, we've been together for three weeks. I might lose my mind around him, but I still have my morals. Give me some credit."

Her slim shoulders lift. "You're right, sorry. But seriously, you're—"

"Glowing," I interject and tug at the neck of my sweater. "I got it."

"Very well, backing off." She unwraps the frilly lace-edged scarf from her neck and looks beyond me toward the menu hanging above the counter. "I'm going to get a hot tea." Her eyes remain firmly set on my face until she's at my back.

Paranoia sets in. *Glowing?* I look at my hands, searching for the glow she speaks of. Nothing. I gaze around Coffee Haven, and no one stares back. The manager, George, chats up Zara as she orders. The gossip ladies are in their usual spot, getting their last batch of gossip in for the year over coffee and scones. Things are normal, for Havenwood Falls, anyway.

"So, where is lover boy? Is he not coming?" Zara asks when she returns to the seat across from me.

"To ice skate at the park? Do you know Breckin at all?"

Her booted foot nudges mine. "Evidently better than you do."

I look up, and there's Breckin, walking by the large picture window and entering the shop. He's dressed in his usual black, a slouchy beanie on his head, and the striped scarf I bought him for Christmas hangs loosely around his neck. He doesn't need those things: hats, scarves, gloves. He doesn't need the jacket or hoodie either. My angel stays warm all on his own, but keeping up appearances when you're a supernatural being is a priority.

His amber-flecked eyes catch mine the moment he's inside, and my stomach flips. He has that power over me. His name alone shoots tingles through my body. The sight of him lights up every nerve ending I own and tightens my core. Maybe I am pregnant. If anyone could get a girl pregnant merely by looking at her, it would be Breckin.

Zara draws a sharp breath. "Viv, you're flickering like those defective tree lights at Napoli's." She touches my hand, and the room turns sideways. "Viv?"

Everything goes fuzzy, and my head becomes too heavy to hold up.

~

"Vivie?" Breckin's breath grazes my ear, his pine-and-snow scent bringing things back into focus. "Hey, are you okay?"

I blink. *What the heck happened?* I'm sitting at Coffee Haven, leaning heavily against a kneeling Breckin, while Zara clutches my hand like a vise. "Did I pass out?"

Breckin's warm hand cups my cheek. "Only for a moment. I walked in and you, well, you just kinda fell forward. I caught you before the table could give you a concussion."

"I fell forward?"

"Are you sure you're feeling okay? That was bloody freaky, Viv. You were—"

"Pale," Breckin interrupts. He reaches across the table and grips Zara's wrist where she still holds my hand. "Viv hasn't eaten today, and had a little sugar crash. She's fine, but maybe you should get her a muffin."

My jaw drops. He's using compulsion.

Zara's dark eyes flare, before Breckin releases her and she stands. "Let me get you a muffin. You should have eaten this morning."

"Chocolate chip," Breckin calls over his shoulder.

"I'm her best friend, Breckin Roberts. I think I know her favorite muffin."

His mouth twists in a subtle smile as he stands and drags Zara's now empty chair closer. "You all right?" he asks, pressing his lips to mine in a chaste kiss that leaves me wanting more.

"I'm fine." I take inventory of my body. Other than the pouting my mouth does at his leaving mine so quickly, everything seems normal. My heart beats, my pulse is steady, my vision is clear, my head pain-free. "The room just sort of flipped on me. I don't know."

I'm back at his side, cuddling into his warmth. *When did I move toward him? What the heck? Crap, I'm practically sitting in his lap. In the coffee shop.* I right myself. The gossip crew will have a field day with our display. Sure enough, Irene Beckett and Laverne and Sybil Carson watch with narrowed eyes.

3

Breckin squeezes my shoulder. "Have you felt okay this morning? Last night?"

"I'm fine," I say, more firmly this time. "What are you doing here, anyway? Yesterday you said it would be a cold day in hell before you spent an afternoon ice skating with a bunch of people in Danzan Park."

His brows raise, probably at my ornery tone. "I changed my mind."

"Why?"

Zara thrusts a sugar-topped muffin in my face, cutting off his reply. "One muffin."

"Thanks, Z," I say, taking the muffin from her hand. I'm not hungry, but who can resist the smell of a freshly baked chocolate chip muffin? I tear the edge off the top and pop it into my mouth. *Thank you, sweet creator of chocolate. So good.*

"Are we going, or what?" Zara picks up her skates. *I guess that's all the time my best friend plans on giving me to recuperate.*

I open my mouth with every intention of backing out, but Breckin beats me to the punch. "Yep, let's go." He stands and grips the back of my chair.

Evidently he's not worried about whatever happened to me when he walked in either. Or he's putting on a show for the benefit of onlookers, and Zara.

"You don't have to come with us, Breckin," I tell him, not for the first time since Zara and I planned this outing a few days ago. He's not big on public spectacles, which is a hard thing to avoid when you live in Havenwood Falls. He's humored me this break with all the town traditions he's allowed me to drag him to.

"Yeah, he does." Zara pins him with her gaze and crosses her arms over her chest. "If you keep finding ways to bail on hanging out with me, Breckin, I'm going to take it personally." A delicately plucked brow curves up, challenging him.

Breckin snorts. "Zara, if I didn't like you, you would know."

She swings her gaze to me. "See, this is why I like him. I like your honesty, Roberts. Let's go take advantage of the December sunshine and have some fun."

Breckin pulls my chair back, picking up my coffee cup as he does. He moves close as I stand and throw the oversized bag carrying my skates over my shoulder. "I told you I wanted you to have normal, remember? If this is your normal, then I'll enjoy it for you."

LIKE THE SQUARE, Danzan Park is full of families enjoying the last day of the year and the sunny winter afternoon. Zara and I have skated at the lake during Christmas break since we were little. It's tradition. When we were too young to come alone, our mothers packed hot chocolate and snacks, and froze their buns off for hours while we twirled around the ice. We liked pretending we were Olympic figure skaters, on our way to golden glory. It didn't matter that neither of us showed much promise; it was fun. It still is.

"I bet I can still spin faster than you," I taunt Zara.

She laughs and glides her way back, stopping next to Breckin, who isn't wearing skates, but is instead standing on the ice in his boots.

"No way. I was always faster," she tells my smirking boyfriend.

"In your dreams. Watch." I skate a small circle and pull my arms and one leg into my body, forcing a spin. The air whistles past my ears. Zara and Breckin's faces whirl by as my revolutions speed up. Around and around, her dark skin, his dark clothing. White snowcapped mountains, then other skaters. The scenery is a blur as I rotate faster and faster.

"Viv, if you break something, I'm gonna laugh." Zara teases, but there's an undercurrent of worry in her words.

Breckin tells me I need to slow down. I scoff. "I do not need to slow down." He growls. "Fine, I'll stop."

I force my arms away from the center of gravity, breaking the aerodynamics and slowing my spin down. Jutting out my foot, I stick my toe pick into the ice with a smile. Then I curtsy, sinking low and lifting my head to three very different faces.

Zara's olive complexion is pale, her mouth wide, her expression confused.

Breckin bites his lip and crosses one arm over his waist. He rubs at his jaw thoughtfully.

The third face I do not recognize, but his eyes cut through me like laser beams. He's beyond the frozen lake, among a crowd of people out enjoying the winter sun. His height and chiseled good looks make him stand out. I study him, my senses on high alert. *He doesn't belong here.* He's dressed for a fashion show—in a camel jacket and turtleneck sweater that look like they were tailored for his wide frame—not a day of fun in the park. *Who is he?*

Breckin touches my arm, and my attention snaps from the unknown man. "Are you dizzy? Because watching you spin like that made *me* dizzy," Breckin jokes, his fingers finding mine.

"You?" I ask. *The angel who flies like he has a death wish?* He chuckles under his breath, and I meet his handsome face with a smile. Then, because I can't help myself, I look around his frame and search for the camel jacket and sweater. The stranger is no longer there. I blink several times, certain I imagined him. "Not dizzy at all," I say breathlessly. "Also, did you freaking growl at me a moment ago?"

With a frown, Breckin looks over his shoulder, then back at me. "Why would I growl at you?" His smile is too wide to be truthful. "Let's go."

Go? I look for Zara. She's already pulling her skates off from where she sits in a pile of snow.

"Where are we going?" I ask as Breckin moves forward. He tugs on my hand, propelling my skates into a glide.

"To my place. We'll drop Zara off at her car behind the square first."

"Why are we—"

"Vivie," he interrupts, "did I tell you to slow down?" he asks, and I stare stupidly. "When you were spinning, did I tell you to slow down?"

"Yes?" My tone is questioning, which is crazy, because he most certainly did. I heard him.

"No. No, I did not. I *thought* it, but I didn't speak it. I also didn't growl at you. Not out loud. I know better." He hurries his steps, dragging me behind him like a sled.

He didn't speak?

"You heard my thoughts, Viv. You also spun inhumanly fast, and you lit up like the Fourth of July when I walked into Coffee Haven earlier. I was going to ignore the angelic glow until later, but the other stuff—" He glances over his shoulder again. "Let's go back to my place, okay?"

I bite my tongue, holding my thoughts as I remove my skates and we walk through the park back to Breckin's Bronco. Zara doesn't protest the abrupt end of our day. *What in the world did he do to her?*

"Are you sure you don't want to go to Rowan's party tonight?" Zara asks, poking her head into the vehicle once we arrive back at the square and she climbs out.

A loud high school party or a quiet night, kissing in the new year with Breckin? *No brainer.* "A Bishop party?" I ask.

"I know it's not normally our thing, but we're seniors. Plus, I don't have a boyfriend to ring in the new year with. Hopefully, I can find a willing participant later."

Oh, my poor boy-crazy friend. Does she resent the place Breckin has taken up in my life in such a short time? I look at Breckin, a silent *Should we go?* plastered on my face.

"Yeah, not happening. Sorry." His tone says he's far from sorry.

Zara rolls her dark eyes with a resigned sigh, like she didn't expect any different. "Whatever. You kids be good then. Keep all that snogging to a minimum."

Breckin's arm stretches along the back of the seats, his fingers combing through my hair. "No promises."

Zara closes the car door with a grumble. "God, I need to find myself a boyfriend."

"Happy New Year, best friend," I call out my open window while she unlocks her car. She flips me off with a laugh as Breckin drives off.

"Okay, let's take it back now." I spit out the words the moment we leave the parking lot. Shifting in my seat, I angle my body Breckin's way. He's so calm. *How is he so calm?* My nails dig into my palms, I'm that freaked. "How did I read your mind? What do you mean I spun inhumanly fast? How in the heck am I glowing? Oh! And, you used compulsion on Z!"

"Vivie, breathe."

"Breathe?" I use the dashboard to brace myself. "I'm pretty sure people are going to question why I'm suddenly a human light bulb, Breckin. Zara already did."

He takes my hand, his fingers weaving between mine.

"Am I a light bulb?" There's a note of humor in his question.

"I'm not what you are," I counter. He doesn't reply. His cheek dents inward, like he's biting it. His silence unnerves me. "Breckin? Do you want to tell me what's going on?"

His shoulders twitch as he pumps my hand in his. I've seen that move before. He's trying to control the angel within. That can't be a good sign.

"What's going on is we're going back to my house, where I get you all to myself for the entire night."

I smile in spite of myself. "You get me to yourself every night, Breck."

The boy lives at my apartment. At first, it was because of the threat looming from the reaper, Sebastian. Now he does it because my mother works nights and he can. Being apart from Breckin is rare, and thanks to our soul connection, that's a good thing. Neither of us handles forced separation well. It's beyond what is normal for two teenagers who began dating three weeks ago. Then again, we're not normal teenagers. He's part angel, and normal went out the window for me on the day I died. Well, died and was brought back to life by his angelic healing.

Breckin removes his hand from mine and adjusts the heater as we turn onto Eleventh. "Yes, but tonight I get you at my place, without having to worry about your mom coming home early from her shift." He holds his hand in front of me, testing the heat blowing from the vent. It's the sort of thing he does without even realizing it. "Did you call her today?"

Frustration wells up at his change of subject, but I indulge him.

For now. "Yeah, earlier, while I was waiting on Zara at Coffee Haven. She's enjoying herself."

"And she's with college friends?" he asks.

I nod. "A few nursing school friends she's kept in touch with, yeah. They get together every year for a girls' weekend in Vegas."

"She trusts you."

"She's never had a reason not to. She's a single mom, so I learned to be responsible at a young age." I catch his small smile out of the corner of my eye. He knows what I'm saying. He didn't have parents growing up. He had nannies, and he had Elias.

"Does she trust me?" he asks.

"You're a guy. Of course she doesn't trust you." I laugh. "But she likes you enough, and she likes Elias. When she left yesterday, she gave me 'the talk.'"

The car slows as we near Breckin's house. "The talk? Vivie, I don't want her to think—"

"She doesn't," I rush to soothe his worry. "Like I said, she trusts me. Breck, my mother got pregnant from a weekend tryst, and the guy disappeared. I've lived with that my entire life. I won't make the same mistake. She knows that."

Breckin sucks in a breath. We turn into his driveway and pull into the garage. It's not until he kills the engine and the garage door closes behind us that he speaks. "You know we're different than that, right? I could never walk away from you. Sex or not."

Talking about sex is awkward. How is it that Zara brought it up earlier, and now Breckin and I are discussing it again? *Note to self: if you can't talk about it without blushing, you should not be doing it.*

"Because we're soul bonded?" I ask, staring out the windshield at the impeccably organized garage wall in front of me.

His fingers touch my chin, turning my face his way. "What do you think?" he asks softly.

I unbuckle myself and wind a hand around his neck, bringing our lips together.

"I think you would never leave me because I'm your favorite couch pillow," I tease against his mouth.

"Something like that," he agrees, pressing his warm lips to mine again and again.

~

BRECKIN'S HOUSE is a mansion compared to the apartment Mom and I live in. It's not as overwhelming as the homes in Havenwood Heights, but the fully renovated and modernized Victorian is expansive and impressive. Since my first visit, we've always spent our time here on the basement level. It's ridiculous to call the space a basement. It has everything we need: bathroom, kitchen, pool room, television, fireplace, comfy sofas. There's even a guest bedroom. Plus, it's underground. In the two weeks since our fight with Sebastian, Breckin hasn't let up his guard. It's like he's worried the reaper told others about us—a Nephilim with a soulmate—and being in the basement eases that worry.

We settle on the couch and watch an action movie marathon. I scoot down low on the seat and prop my blanket-covered legs on the footrest. Breckin sprawls out lengthwise with his head on my lap—I *am* his favorite pillow—and his feet hanging over the opposite arm rest.

"Have you seen your father since that night?" I ask randomly, halfway into movie two during a commercial break.

His attention turns from the television, stilling the hand I've been running through his smooth angelic hair. He shakes his head in the negative as he turns in my lap. "I would have told you if I had."

"Would you?" I ask, twirling a chunk of his bangs around my index finger.

"Viv?"

I push at his head. "You changed the subject in the car, and you're not telling me everything. What are you worried about?"

He pulls himself into a sitting position and combs his fingers through his mussed hair. "I don't *know* anything. Yes, I'm worried. I'm worried that Hamon will try to take you from me. That another reaper will appear, that something else might want you, like Sebastian did."

His shoulders rise with a deep inhale. "Vivie, I'm worried I hurt you when I healed you, and we just don't know the repercussions yet. Then there's my eighteenth birthday and what that will mean for me, for you, for us." He scrubs his hand over his face, and his shoulders drop. "Elias is keeping things from me."

I pull my legs in and set my feet on the floor. My arms and hands reach for Breckin, drawing him close, until he's the one wrapping me in a hug.

"I'm sorry," I murmur into his neck. "You don't have to keep it to yourself. I'm part of this now. Let me in."

His hold tightens. "You're a high school senior. This is not what you need to deal with."

"So are you," I remind him, and he exhales. "I know, you're not normal, but guess what, Breck? Neither am I. Not anymore."

We separate, and my fingers go to my hair, twirling the ends nervously.

Breckin shakes his head with a grin. "No, you're not. You were glowing today, like an angel. I think my healing you did something. Changed you somehow."

"You saved my life and made me your soul mate, but the downside is I might be a human night-light?" When put in perspective, can I complain? So, I might glow occasionally. I could be dead.

"Elias trained me to control it, to mask it, when I was young. Maybe he could train you, too. We'll figure this out, but not tonight, Vivie." He gives my knee a squeeze, his amber eyes scanning my face. "Hey, you wanna go see the fireworks in a way you never have?"

I release my fear. He's so earnest. So worried about providing me with normal experiences, as though he's to blame for where we are now. "With you? Of course."

We take to the sky, leaving crowds and traffic jams to the humans. Every New Year's Eve Mount Mae Ski Resort has a torchlight parade down the blue square slope, Renae's Way. I've been many times, but never like this—never hidden in the sky, in the arms of an angel. From up here, the mountain appears like it's on fire. Skiers weave their way back and forth, the flames in their hands lighting the path, creating a radiance that steals your breath.

"It's pretty amazing, huh?" Breckin whispers in my ear.

"It's gorgeous," I agree. "This is why you love flying so much, isn't it? Everything is beautiful from up here. Lights look romantic, streets seem peaceful, the air is clean."

His wings stretch out, bringing us higher and moving us away from the slopes. "I used to love it because it cleared my head. Like running for you."

Like running *was* for me. Since the attack, I haven't been able to run. Haven't wanted to.

"You said used to," I point out, as below us the crowd erupts in a countdown.

His warm nose nudges the side of my face, pulling my attention from the ground to his eyes. "Isn't it obvious? I don't need to clear my mind the way I used to. When I'm stressed, I have you."

"Aw, of course you would say sweet things when I don't dare move."

Breckin laughs as a cannon pops in the distance. "I'll be sure to repeat myself when we're on the ground, then," he says, his leg hooking around mine tightly as he turns toward the north. Sparks ignite the sky, sizzling and popping in brilliant flashes.

"Happy New Year, Vivie."

Lifting my face to his, I smile as his eyes light up in a rainbow of colors. "Happy New Year, Breck," I say, my lips brushing his.

WHEN THE TRUTH HUNTS YOU DOWN

BRECKIN

*W*e float to the ground with our mouths fused together. Vivienne's hands slip around my neck the moment our feet touch solid surface.

"I meant what I said earlier," I murmur against her lips. "We'll figure things out."

"Shh." Her fingers grip my hair.

With hungry mouths and searching hands, we celebrate the new year cloaked from the crowd in town square. Kissing her is like touching a live wire. There isn't a cell in my body that doesn't come alive when we're connected this way. Her soft lips tease mine, and the wildly erotic rhythm of our kiss has my hands drawing her closer and closer. I long to devour every part of this girl. When the last firework fizzles out and the crowd noise picks up, we part. My breathing is ragged, and Vivienne's lips are swollen, her flushed face owed more to our kissing than the cold.

"Ready to go back to my place?" I tug her crocheted hat over her ears.

She nods and glances around the square. Most people are packing up their chairs and thermoses and heading home, but a few linger.

"Hot chocolate and a roaring fire, right?"

"Of course. Anything for my human popsicle."

She slaps my side. "You know, I'm not nearly as cold as I thought—"

"Viv," I interrupt, as a spasm runs up my spine and along my wings. They're agitated. "We need to go."

Her spine stiffens beneath the hand I have at her back. She turns her head my way, her eyes both curious and concerned.

"Someone, some*thing*, is here." I have us cloaked from sight, but against another angel, it's useless. I grab Vivienne's waist and pull her in as I search the vicinity, looking for someone who shouldn't be here. Havenwood Falls has many supes to distinguish among. My powers aren't as sharp as Elias's, which makes pinpointing the exact nature or location of a threat more difficult.

Vivienne wraps her arms securely around my back, but I hesitate as a faint angelic shimmer catches my eye. It moves with the crowd away from our position, then stops as though it knows it has been spotted. The sea of people between us part, and there he stands: an angel with sharp, coffee colored wings.

"He's an angel," Vivienne says on a hitched breath, her fingers digging into my skin. "He was at the park today."

"Hang on." I jump into the air, my wings pumping as quickly as I dare when I have Vivienne with me. Her head tucks into my warm skin, and I hold tight while my mind contemplates what just happened.

"You saw the angel?" I ask, needing confirmation.

"Brown wings, cropped blond hair, marble-chiseled jawline?" She clings to me, her warm breath tickling my chest. "Yeah, I saw the angel."

Whoever he was, he doesn't seem to be following us.

"Breck? Where are we going?" Vivienne asks when I overshoot my house and keep heading north.

"I want to talk with Elias."

"Now?"

The changes happening within her line up like toy soldiers. "Right now."

14

~

WE CIRCLE SKI-VENTURES' hangar, and when I'm sure it's safe, I land on the gravel sidewalk to the front office door. Elias lives in the space above the office. Except for his usual spotlights on the property, the building is dark.

"I'm sure he's sleeping," Vivienne says, her hand tugging on mine. "Can't we call him in a few hours?"

"You know angels don't sleep, Vivie." She frowns. Why is she so hesitant? That isn't like her at all. "What's wrong?"

"Nothing." She kicks at the gravel, releasing my hand and turning in a circle. *She's full of crap.*

"I am not full of crap, thank you very much," she hisses. I nearly lose my footing as she rounds on me. "It's just that when you say we need Elias that means bad things are happening and"—she gathers her windblown hair and sweeps it to one side, twisting it around her hand— "well, I was kind of hoping we could start the new year without any bad things."

She's so beautiful, with her angry eyes and disgruntled pout. I can't stop my smile as I wait for her to stomp a foot. "Uh, Vivie, bad things don't exactly follow our timelines."

"Really, Breckin Roberts?" She snatches a rock from the ground and hurls it at me, hitting my shoulder.

"Nice throw."

"Don't be smug." She does stomp her foot this time. "I just . . . I don't get it."

"You read my mind again." I point out what she didn't realize on her own.

She stills. "I did?"

"Yes. I didn't actually say you were full of crap out loud." She grabs at her hair, her fingers returning to their nervous habit of twisting. "You also saw an angel who was cloaked."

"That's not unusual. I've been able to see you when you're cloaked."

I tuck my wings away and remove my shirt from my waistband,

pulling it over my head. "Elias and I assumed you saw me because of our bond. You didn't see him when he followed you just last week. So—"

She raises her hand. "Hold up. Why was Elias following me last week?"

"Because I can't follow you all the time. He helps out."

"That's creepy, Breckin. I don't want him following me around incognito. I don't need you following me around all the time either. If you want to be around me, just tell me."

I close the space between us and take hold of the collar of her jacket. "Vivie, I always want to be around you, but I can't. I need breaks." She has no idea how intense the emotions she brings out in me are. Or, maybe she does, but she's human. She's always dealt with feelings like these. Elias said my emotions as a Nephilim are half of what a human's are.

Drawing her closer, I drop my forehead to the top of hers. "My reactions to you are too strong. I send Elias to keep you safe when I can't."

The tips of her fingers brush my cheek. She's wearing fingerless mittens, and though her hands should be cold in this weather, they're warm.

"Why are your reactions too strong?" she asks softly.

I smile. It's an insanely human thing—to love. But I know no other word for what I feel.

"You know the answer to that," I tell her, unable to say the three words. Not yet.

She lifts to her toes and presses a simple kiss to my mouth.

ELIAS ISN'T HOME. He spends much of his time wandering Havenwood Falls, keeping an eye on things. He's been unusually jumpy the last few weeks. Even before the stuff with Vivienne, he was concerned about things going on in town. He ordered me to remain home over Thanksgiving weekend due to rumblings of demons and angels nearby.

"We'll wait," I say as I unlock his office and let us in. Vivienne drags herself through the door unhappily. "He doesn't have a fireplace, but I bet he has hot chocolate," I tease, touching her lower back as we walk inside.

Elias does have hot chocolate—the expensive kind, too. Vivienne squeals with delight when she finds marshmallows to toss in. This girl and her love of sugar. We settle on his large couch upstairs and turn on the television. Vivienne relaxes into the crook between my arm and shoulder, her back pressed to my chest.

"You're not freaking out as much as I thought you would," I say after a while, when she hasn't fallen asleep.

"You mean because I'm apparently developing superpowers and there's an angel in town who may or may not be after me?"

Crap.

"You're not developing superpowers, Vivie."

She lifts the arm I have resting over her waist and sits up. "But I may have another angel after me?"

I scoot into a sitting position, my back in the corner of the couch. "I don't know. That's why we're here."

"And the glowing, mind reading, super speed—"

"That would be your angelic heritage coming to life," a familiar voice says behind us.

We turn in our seats and find Elias standing in the doorway.

"I didn't expect to come home to find two teens crashing my place." His eyes are shadowed by his ever-present baseball cap, but they survey every aspect of the scene before him. A father's eyes, only they're narrowed in on me, like I'm the dirty teenage boy longing to spoil his precious princess. He's not wrong. I move my hand from her thigh. "It's past two a.m., Breckin. Shouldn't Viv be at home in her own bed?"

Vivienne stills, her eyes glued to the doorway even as Elias walks farther into the space. He just dropped a bomb and he's lecturing me on curfew?

"As you obviously overheard, we were waiting on you," I point out.

He rests his forearms on the back of a chair at a right angle to the couch, and I spy the twitching of his lips.

"Stop playing the menacing father figure, you ass. You'll scare Viv with that ugly scowl."

Vivienne grabs my shin as she whirls on the couch and faces Elias. "I'm sorry, did you just say . . . I mean . . ." She falters, her mind grappling with what he said when he walked in.

I pull my legs from behind Vivienne and sit beside her.

"What did you mean by angelic heritage?" I ask as politely as possible, considering I want to throw something heavy at his head. What has he kept from me?

Elias shrugs a shoulder. "I may have lied to you."

Shit. "May have?" I ask tersely.

"Okay, I lied to you."

Son of a— I inhale through my nose, slowly, deliberately. A fire smolders within my chest. Angelic anger ignited. My human temper isn't much better. Vivienne's leg touches mine from socked foot up to our hips. Having her near only stokes the fire.

Elias rounds the chair and perches on the edge. Removing his cap, he scratches at his bearded cheeks and levels his gaze on me. "Your father and I didn't technically fall, Breckin. We left."

"You *left* Heaven? Why?" I ask.

"Because," he sighs heavily, "we loved her more than we loved Him."

The world pauses. "Her?"

His watery blue gaze slides to Vivienne. "Phaedra."

Beside me, Vivienne gasps, and my arm snakes around her back automatically as recognition dawns on her face.

I catch Elias's nod in my peripheral view. "Yes," he says, his voice dropping lower than usual.

Her fingers toy with her lower lip. "You loved her more than . . . him?" she murmurs.

"Him." His brows lift as he nods again.

My fingers touch Vivienne's lower back, whether to ground myself or her, who knows?

"What am I missing?" I ask, my gaze going between the two of them.

I'm hit with a cacophony of emotions when Vivienne turns toward me. Every thought she seems to be having tries drilling its way into my head.

"Damn." Clutching my forehead, I clench my eyes.

"Viv, calm down," Elias says after a moment. More words and images hammer me. "You're projecting your thoughts to Breckin, and he can't take that all in. Take deep breaths, and calm down."

Her presence at my side disappears, and I open my eyes as she argues with Elias.

"I don't know how! What am I doing?" she asks desperately, her feet inching away from me.

Holy hell! I reach for her.

"Vivie, listen to him." I barely recognize my own voice. Blinking rapidly, like batting my damn eyes will diminish the thoughts bombarding their way into my head like a battering ram, I hold her gaze. "You're on overload."

Her hands wrap around mine. "Okay, okay. I'm breathing. I'm calming," she says with a grimace. "It's just, Phaedra was the first in our family to come to Havenwood Falls. My great great, I don't know how many greats, grandmother."

With that revelation, her thoughts turn down a notch.

"Tell me more about her," I say, maintaining eye contact with Vivienne and ignoring Elias's form now hovering beyond her left shoulder. "Get it out. It's helping."

"Oh." Her eyes widen. "Well, I don't know much about her. I've never known much about my family history. My mom's dad was a hippie who left the area not long after she was born. Her mom died when she was a teen, some strange illness. It's why she went to school for medicine."

I cock my head sideways as a rhythmic thumping slows within my body. No, not in my body—in Vivienne's. Her heartbeat. I hear it, feel it like it is my own. My wings shoot out, propelling me forward and into the coffee table as Elias and Vivienne are knocked back.

"Breckin?" Vivienne cries out, startled.

At the same time Elias curses, "What the hell!"

I pull the traitors tightly to my back and sidle away from the table, careful not to damage anything. When I'm in open space, they spring to full width again. They suddenly have a mind of their own.

"Your heart—" I gasp. It's racing again, from the shock of my wings appearing, I assume. I press my hand to my chest and glance at Elias. "I feel the beating of her heart."

Vivienne's hand mimics mine, covering her heart as she sinks into the back cushions of the couch. A small smile touches her lips.

"What about your wings, Breckin?" Elias asks.

"Did you hear what I said? I feel—"

"What about your wings?" His gruff voice asks for a second time. "You didn't sense me come home, and your wings are thinking on their own. Your father said you needed training."

My hand falls to my side. "*Hamon* implied I needed to be a better fighter. Since I have no intention of fighting for him . . ." I shrug.

Elias stalks me across the room, his face wild.

"Don't say that out loud," he warns. His gaze darts around. Does he think we're being watched? Listened to? "Your *father* was speaking of more than physical fighting. Your angel side needs to be stronger for what's to come."

"And what is that?" We both turn at Vivienne's cool voice. Whatever it was that caused so much chaos in her mind has left. She's poised, if a little unsure, as she rises to her feet. "It's time you tell us both the truth. What is coming, and what does it have to do with Phaedra?"

MADE FOR THIS

VIVIENNE

"Can you put those things away?" Elias asks Breckin with not a small amount of exasperation. "I'll get you a shirt."

Breckin nods and rolls his neck. His nose bunches up, like he's straining to hide the huge feathered appendages on his back. After a moment, they finally blink out of existence. Breckin rubs the back of his neck as he turns sideways to me. No wonder he needs a new shirt —the back of his is shredded, thanks to the unexpected appearance of his wings.

"Are you all right?"

My gaze slides from ogling his muscles and abs to his face.

"Huh?" I ask, a little breathless. *Oh, what this angel does to me.*

"Your cheek?" He brushes my skin tenderly with his knuckles, a knowing look working its way into his eyes.

"I . . ." My fingers circle his wrist. "Those weapons in your back pack a swift punch." What I meant as a tease erases the small smile I just saw light up his eyes. His face falls. "Breck, I'm fine. It was an accident." I move in and hug him tightly, my hands easily creeping between the torn pieces of cotton to touch his warm skin.

"Here," Elias says. Breckin's arm shoots into the air and catches the shirt tossed at his head. Kissing my forehead, he steps back and pulls what's left of his shirt from his body, replacing it with a new, slightly too big Havenwood Falls Ski-Ventures shirt.

"It's been a while since I've thrown away clothing due to unruly wings." Breckin laughs, but Elias isn't amused, and I'm worried.

When he's done, he takes my hand and draws me near once more, kissing my temple. "By the way, you have no idea what you do to me."

I pull my head back, my cheeks flaming. *This mind reading thing is going to be a pain in the—*

Breckin's finger touches my lips, as though he can stop me from thinking my thoughts.

Damn you! He laughs at my outburst and squeezes me tighter.

Elias returns to his chair, and we settle on the couch. Breckin clears his throat. "Okay, I think we need to begin with Viv's grandmother. Phaedra."

Elias nods.

Breckin repeats Elias's earlier revelation. Hamon and Elias were not forced from Heaven as they'd led Breckin to believe all these years. They'd left. "What you're telling me is that my father, the angel who hates mankind, was so in love with a human that he left Heaven to be here with her?"

I'm no expert, but the full-blooded angel in the room looks uncomfortable. His shoulders rise and fall before he speaks. "Phaedra wasn't human, Breckin."

"Phaedra wasn't human?" I repeat, like that will make it sink in. *That would be your angelic heritage coming to life.* I gasp as his earlier words sink in. "All of the changes . . . I'm not becoming like Breckin, I'm becoming . . ."

"Who you were meant to be," Elias finishes for me.

When I was little, Mom bought me a porcelain Christmas angel doll. She had curly platinum locks and large blue eyes, and held a candle in her movable arms. I plugged her in and watched for hours as her little arms opened and closed, and her head dipped from side-to-side. I twirled her curls around my chubby childish fingers and told stories about her angelic life. About the angel she loved who left her at my home while he saved people . . .

Sniffing, I pop out of the memory and focus like mad on keeping my thoughts in check. Breckin and Elias carry on a conversation that I've completely lost track of.

"I don't understand," Breckin says. "If Viv's ancestor is an angel, shouldn't she be like me? Wouldn't her mom?"

"It's more complicated than that." Elias looks between us. "I'd hoped Hamon would be the one to share the story someday. He's not exactly what you think, Breckin."

"You mean, he's not a fallen angel who abandoned his unwanted offspring to his best friend and only stopped by to threaten me with a future I do not want?" Breckin asks angrily. My heart crumbles at the vulnerability Breckin's showing. "If your story is meant to explain away his cruelty, I'm not interested."

Breckin pops to his feet, and I reach for his hand a moment too late as he pads across the room and disappears into the bedroom. I push up from the couch to go after him.

"Let him be," Elias sighs.

"No." That one word comes out with a defiance I didn't know I had. "Maybe that is how you've dealt with him through the years, but that's not how I will deal with him. Not when he's hurting."

"He doesn't know what he's feeling."

"Maybe not by name, but he feels something."

Breckin's explained his human and angel emotions to me. The way they push and pull for power. Sometimes he isn't sure which side of him is making decisions. He isn't one person, not in his mind. He is to me.

"You know, I don't care what side is struggling, Elias. He is Breckin. He's mine. My soul mate, my love. I can't let him hurt."

I'm barely around the coffee table when Elias's words stop me. "You are so like her. Probably the most like her of any of her offspring."

My shoulders stiffen. I look toward the doorway through which Breckin disappeared and will my legs to go to him, but my feet turn back toward Elias.

"You knew them? My ancestors?"

The rugged lines around his eyes soften as he nods. "Some better than others. Phaedra was soft and full of love. It was her downfall, Viv—her open heart."

Something damp trails down my cheek. I refuse to accept that I've shed a tear. "Are you saying it will be my downfall too?"

The barest of smiles cracks beneath his unruly beard. He needs a good trim. "Not at all," he says, looking beyond me. "I'm hoping your soft heart will save them."

"Them?" I turn toward where his gaze lingers and find Breckin leaning against the doorframe watching me. *Does he mean you?*

Breckin confirms my unspoken question with a slight incline of his head. "And Hamon," he adds, lifting a brow for Elias's verification.

"I kept things from you both, for many reasons. Viv, until Breckin saved you, there was no reason for you to know about your bloodline. Even after he saved you, I wasn't sure if you needed to know. I had no idea what his healing powers would do. The soul mate bond could have been the same as when humans bond."

"And now?"

"The changes you've noticed are angelic qualities. Maybe if you were a normal human girl, you'd still develop them, to a lesser degree."

If you were a normal human girl. My throat closes at the implication, the reminder that I am, in fact, not normal anymore.

"Breathe." I jump at Breckin's voice spoken so clearly in my mind.

I glare at him across the room as my pulse soars. "Geez, don't do that."

"That"—Elias laughs and waves his hand between us—"is what I'm talking about. You two hear each other in your minds. Your bond is strong."

My thoughts bubble up, trying to take over, and I push them back down. No way will I send this mess to Breckin to deal with. Breckin's wink tells me he knows exactly what I'm doing, but he's not writhing in pain, so while he might be receiving some of my random musings, I must be channeling most of it away from him.

"So Viv is part angel, but she's not a Nephilim?"

"No. Technically she would be, but Phaedra was stripped of her angelic markers before she had a child." Breckin and I share a confused look, and Elias scratches at his head as he explains. "Phaedra lived as a human with angelic blood that was . . . well, we never knew what exactly happened. I suppose you could say it was asleep all this time."

"And my healing Viv woke it up? That is what the reaper recognized in her almost immediately. He saw her angelic DNA," Breckin guesses.

Elias nods. "It makes the most sense."

"You lied to me. When Sebastian came after her, when we discussed her parents—"

"You discussed my parents?" It's my turn to be angry. Breckin's never asked about my father. "You know nothing about my parents. How could you discuss them?"

Breckin comes to my side and takes my hands. "Vivie, we were discussing your bloodline. Angels sense things, like DNA. You have a . . . different scent I never could identify. I thought it was because of our bond." He looks at Elias. "You knew, though. You knew she had angelic blood, and you lied about it."

Elias doesn't look guilty as much as he looks sorry. Breckin trusts him implicitly, and knowing Elias kept things from him can't be easy. I long to slink from the room to allow them time to discuss it all. Then it hits me. They're talking about things that pertain to me. This isn't about them alone. Not anymore.

With his eyes trained on my face, Breckin rolls his shoulders back and stiffens as he asks, "Does he know?"

Silence hangs before Elias's baritone answers, "He does."

"I'd like for you both to stop speaking about things like I'm not here." My gaze flicks between them. Elias opens his mouth, and I hold up my hand. "No. I am no longer a human girl; you said so yourself. Include me."

"Viv, I have watched over your line since the 1800s. That has been my job on earth, given to me by your father, Breckin."

"Oh, no." My eyes cross as the association hits me. "Hamon loved Phaedra. They weren't . . . they didn't—"

A strangled groan of denial dances through my head—Breckin's voice. I sink back to the couch, my gut churning. Understanding dawns on Elias's face.

"You two are not related," he assures us. The knot in my stomach releases. "Phaedra married a human man, and they settled here in Havenwood Falls not long after it was founded."

"Why did you watch over her?" I ask.

"She was an angel without angelic powers. We knew she would be hunted once they discovered what she was."

The snarl of an angry animal echoes in my ears. My hand goes to my ribcage, the sting of an injury since healed returning. *Hunted.* "They?"

"The legions of damned," Breckin replies.

Flashes of white appear in my vision as the blood drains from my face. "I think I'm going to be sick," I murmur, getting to my feet.

Breckin's at my side instantly, one hand at my elbow and the other around my back as he ushers me toward the bathroom. I feel Elias's presence following us, but I close my eyes and breathe through my nose. The lid to the toilet hits the porcelain tank, and I open my eyes. Worried faces stare at me.

"Are you both going to hold my hair and watch if I throw up?"

Elias backs out of the bathroom, but Breckin remains. "Are you okay?" he asks, tucking my hair behind my ear.

I nod. "Just, give me a moment." I sit on the cold edge of the bathtub and lower my head between my knees.

Breckin's legs appear in my view as he kneels and takes my hands, rubbing them. "What happened?"

"You were right," I manage between deep inhales and exhales. "I don't want to deal with this stuff. I just want to enjoy our senior year. Maybe graduate high school, go to college, have a few dates with my boyfriend." I raise my eyes, looking up at him through a curtain of hair.

"Vivie." The two syllables roll off his tongue with such sadness, my limbs ache with it.

"Is the entire world like this? Angels and . . . and what? Demons? What else is out there?"

He gives my hands a squeeze and stands. "We're done for tonight. Let's go back to my house."

"Done?" my weak voice asks. We can't be done. I have far too many questions for that. Another dizzy spell washes in and prevents me from arguing. Once again, I close my eyes and breathe.

"There was an angel watching us tonight, and Viv saw him today, too," Breckin whispers in the hallway. "He could have followed us, but he didn't."

Elias grunts. "He could have been an angel passing by. Maybe he sensed you, or Viv, and became curious."

"Do you feel the difference?" Breckin asks, softer this time.

I remain hunched over on my bathtub perch, my head hanging low, my hair covering my face—my ears wide open. *Difference?*

Elias's whispered reply stops my breath. "Something is off."

I hold the air in my lungs, waiting for more. My heart slams against my ribcage, filling my ears and making them difficult to hear. I pick up bits and pieces as they fade further away.

". . . not Phaedra . . . not you either," Elias's deeper tone says.

Breckin mumbles.

Releasing my breath, I open one eye. They're no longer in the hallway outside the bathroom door. I stretch my legs in front of me, then pull them back in and stand. I poke my head out and don't see them. *Dang angels.*

The nausea has passed. Twisting my hair around my hand, I throw it behind my back, turn on the faucet, and splash water on my face. The dark shadows beneath my eyes and my sallow complexion stand out. I'm exhausted. Flipping off the light, I shuffle back toward Elias's living space. *Where did they go?*

I'm about to collapse on the couch when Breckin appears through a second doorway off the main space.

"Let me check—" he's saying over his shoulder when he turns and spots me standing there. With a smile he walks to my side. "Sorry I disappeared. Elias wants us to stay here tonight, considering . . . We were making the bed."

Considering an unknown angel was following us today? Considering

I'm different? That I'm part angel? Changing? I ask the questions with more than a little sarcasm in my mind, but Breckin doesn't hear a word, and I don't care to ask out loud.

"That's fine, lead the way," I say instead.

∽

BRECKIN TURNS his back as I slip off my pants and settle into bed wearing only my underwear and the long-sleeved shirt I had on under the sweater I removed. The bed is made with simple white sheets, a blue blanket, and a thick downy white comforter. The headboard is nearly hidden by a mound of pillows.

"Are you staying?" I ask Breckin as I shift and sort through the pillows until I find the perfect one.

"If you want me to."

Rolling to my side, I sigh. "What a stupid answer, Breckin Roberts."

A moment later, the bed sinks with his weight and the heat of my angel envelops me, folding and bending with my body until we are one. While one arm wraps under my shoulders and hugs my chest, the other remains at my stomach. He's careful not to touch the skin exposed by my being pantless. It's sweet, and I wrap my arms around his with a content sigh.

"Do you think Elias will tell us the story behind Phaedra and how they all came to be here if we ask?" I wonder out loud.

"I honestly don't know."

"Have you spoken to him about your father?" I ask cautiously. Breckin's fingers press against my skin in response. "He seems pretty adamant that there are things you don't know, Breck. Things you should know."

A low grumble plays in his throat before he speaks. "What I know is Hamon left me, Vivie. He left me here with a string of human nannies and Elias as family. I didn't meet him until I was ten. Did I tell you that? I have a hard time believing anything he says now could change my feelings."

28

Breckin likes to pretend he's not bitter. That Hamon, and what he did, or didn't do, does not matter to him. But it does, and in the darkness of night, he sometimes allows those emotions out. He swallows hard, and my body recognizes the tensing of his muscles at my back.

"He left paradise for her. He followed some angel to Earth, risking his eternity, but he couldn't be bothered to see his son."

My eyes burn. "Oh, Breckin." I attempt turning in his arms, offering comfort, but he tightens his hold and buries his face in my hair.

"It's not like Elias didn't try, you know . . . but I knew. I knew he was out there and not here."

Righteous indignation fills me. I understand his pain. I was a fatherless child, too, but Mom made it clear from early on that the man who left her me as a present was not someone I wanted to know. She was ashamed of herself, of that story, but the truth was she didn't know him beyond one night. And that one night changed her life. I understand that now, too. How one moment, one encounter, has the power to alter the course of your entire life.

I cling to him, holding him as tightly as he holds me until his emotions calm. His breaths slow and smooth out. His muscles relax. After a few minutes, he nudges the back of my head with his nose. I bend my neck forward, giving him access to my nape.

"Are you freaked out about it all?" His lips graze my skin with each word.

I pull my knees closer into my chest, and his follow, staying directly behind like a second skin. "Let's see, from an animal left you for dead, to a reaper wants you, to your angel DNA was suddenly woken up by my magic hands—I'd say tonight's news is easier to swallow than the other secrets you've shared with me."

A light huff of hot air tickles the baby-fine hair at my hairline.

"Are you laughing at me?" I pinch the arm he has wrapped around my stomach.

"With you?" he asks, as he plants another kiss on me.

29

I crane my neck, trying to look over my shoulder, and his mouth ends up at the shell of my ear. "You're not worried, are you?" I ask.

Breckin wiggles his arm out from underneath my body and rolls me over till we're eye to eye. The room is dark, with the exception of a sliver of light from the cracked-open door. *Did Elias, in a fit of fatherly protectiveness, tell him to leave it open?*

"Vivie." He cups my cheek. "I told you earlier, I will always worry about you, but tonight gave me hope I didn't have before."

"Why is that?"

"Tonight I learned the girl I gave my soul to, the girl I love, isn't human."

All but one word fades into a black abyss the moment he says it. Love. L-O-V-E.

"You love me?" My voice cracks. "I thought it was too soon and too ridiculous to say those words," I admit, my hand working up his chest until the beating of his heart is a song beneath my palm.

"Now *that* is a ridiculous thing to say."

His admonishment drags a light giggle from my lips. "I love you, too, Breckin."

His head slides closer on the pillow we share. "I know."

Our lips meet, brushing with the soft tentative first strokes of paint meeting canvas. We ease into the kiss knowing full well the fury that love and desire creates when our mouths connect. I love kissing Breckin. When we begin, his tender and easy hands sweep over my skin like a blind man reading braille. By the time we pull apart, my scalp stings from where he's tugged my hair through his fingers, and my chin is chafed from the light stubble on his. But it's only kissing. Two mouths moving in sync in a way that promises more. Eventually.

"You should sleep." He smooths my hair back and kisses me once more. A gentle peck.

"You know, if I'm going to acquire all these angelic powers, the least they could do is give me your never needing to sleep power."

Breckin rolls to his back with a chuckle. "My 'never needing to sleep' power? And who exactly do you think *they* are?"

I snuggle into his side with my face in the crook of his shoulder and chest. "I don't know. *They*. Whoever it is that doles these things out." I gasp and shoot into a sitting position. "Oh my gosh. I'm not human?"

Breckin pushes onto his elbow. "You catch on quick," he says through a wide smile.

"Am I? Could I?" I can't voice my thoughts quick enough. *Angelic powers.*

Breckin rescues me. "Vivie, why do you think I said I have hope now that I know you're not human?" When I don't move, his hand grasps the back of my shirt and tugs. I allow him to draw me back into his side. "Do you know what plagues me the most? It's wondering how I am supposed to live a life watching from afar as my soul mate lives hers."

Desolation returns to his tone, and I roll to my stomach and prop myself up on my elbows, whispering his name.

"I wasn't worried about it right now, but later . . . five, ten years from now, you were going to keep going, and I would be stuck here."

"You're immortal, aren't you?" I had wondered, but was too afraid to ask. His dark silhouette nods, and I take a deep breath. "You have hope now that I could be, too?"

I'm a logical girl. I read romance novels and like fairy tales, but I've never known much about supernatural beings. I've never studied the stories of angels, whether fiction or nonfiction. What would immortality mean? A lifetime with Breckin, but what about other things? Children? Mom? A normal life wouldn't be possible. What may seem like a gift feels like a possible curse.

He tugs my hair to regain my attention. "And you don't." It's not a question.

"Immortality," I say in a low whisper. "I don't know what that means. One moment I'm a girl . . ." The thought doesn't finish.

"Do you remember what Elias said when he first told us we're soul mates?"

I tuck up under his jaw and curve my body around his side.

31

Closing my eyes, I repeat Elias's words. "It's a powerful connection and most people consider it a gift from the maker."

"To fulfill the order of things," he finishes when I purposefully leave that part out. "We have a destiny, Vivie."

Breckin remembers Elias's comments on destiny, and I remember the reaper Sebastian's words the night he tried to take me from Breckin on the mountainside.

"Will she join you?" he'd asked Breckin, his electric blue eyes burning holes into mine. "Will she turn her back on her calling for you?"

Two words: destiny and calling.

Two parts: human and angel.

What if the two don't go hand in hand?

WITHOUT YOU

BRECKIN

"*F*estival of Lights?" I text Viv during English Lit the following Monday when we return to school.

From the moment we woke mid-morning on January first to the smell of bacon and pancakes at Elias's to the ride to school this morning, she's refused to discuss Phaedra.

When we returned to my house last Monday, we spent the day curled up on the couch in the basement with the lights out and the fire burning. I'd bring the subject up and she'd shush me.

"I want to enjoy our last day without my mom being home," she said between kisses. "She's going to want to spend tomorrow with me. Let's be in the now."

With her fingers digging into the hair at the back of my head and her mouth teasing mine, I had no power to resist.

Things have remained settled. No lightbulb Vivienne, no mind reading, no angels following us. We've had one week of normal. I knock my knuckles on the wooden top of my desk.

Her texted reply comes back twenty minutes later, right before the bell. "Yes?"

She's such a rule follower. She probably didn't remove her phone from her pocket until her teacher finished whatever their lesson was. I don't bother replying as the bell rings.

Weaving through the narrow halls of Havenwood Falls High is an adventure in supernatural species. I pick up the scent of every creature living among the humans. The perfume of teenage hormones and a hundred different blood types can be nauseating, but I've learned to live with it. My ability to hear things is more frustrating. There's nothing like sitting in class working on an essay test and picking up on a little supply-closet rendezvous between two of your teachers.

I catch Vivienne's laughter when I come to where our two hallways intersect, and I stop. Cocking my head, I determine she's still halfway down the hall. I lean against a bank of lockers and wait. Her lilting laugh tugs at my lips, and I search through the crowd to catch a glimpse of her shining hair. Instead, I find myself grinning stupidly at Kai Reynolds. The arrogant vampire lifts a brow and checks over his shoulder. He must spot Vivienne because when he turns back, his face clearly says *you're whipped, man* as he passes by. Tossing my head back, I acknowledge him, and he offers me a subtle nod in return. That's the extent of our friendship—nods and the occasional lazy comment about life.

Half the Kasun pack follows behind Kai, cutting up and jostling one another, and then Vivienne rounds the corner. At barely over five feet, Vivienne and Cressida Manos, the annoyingly cheerful mountain nymph she's with, were overshadowed by the rowdy wolves.

I wade into the sea of students and come up at Vivienne's side. "Fancy meeting you here."

"Breckin, hey." Vivienne's freshly coated pink lips spread into a wide smile.

Cressida's green eyes volley between us. "So, you two are really an item?" the junior asks as though she's surprised.

"We really are," I deadpan and take Vivienne's hand in mine. "Are you surprised this goddess gave me the time of day?" I ask the nymph.

Red flames to match her red hair color Cressida's cheeks. "No, no. I think you two are perfect together. Some might say a match made in heaven." She abruptly turns into the classroom on the right with a wink and a wave.

Vivienne's warm eyes pop wide. "Did she just—" Her steps slow.

A body bounces off my shoulder as students shove around us, cursing. We're an idle boat in the middle of a busy channel.

"Keep moving with the current." I tug Vivienne's hand.

"So, the Festival of Lights?" I ask to distract her from Cressida's little tease.

Vivienne frowns. "What about it?"

Her eyes cloud over as she mumbles beneath her breath. Her mind is in a whole other place.

Looking at the students around us, I take a breath and lean closer. "I thought we could go."

Vivienne huffs, once again slamming on her brakes in the middle of the hall. A white-haired guy skids to a stop before he runs into her back. Tarron Wilde, he's an elf . . . with witch blood. I shrug a silent apology for the roadblock as he meets my eyes, then steps around us.

"That was weird, right?" Vivienne asks.

"Nope, it's not weird at all. You're blocking the hall."

Her eyes look at me, but they aren't *looking* at me. "I mean, she winked. She called us a match . . ." Her fingers foray to the ends of her hair. Twisting.

At any moment now, the bell will ring for next period, and here we are, stuck in the main hall, with her fixating on Cressida's comment and me completely failing in my effort to ask her on a date. It shouldn't be this hard. Should it? Frustrated, I pull her hand and drag her toward an alcove a few feet away.

"Breckin," she hisses. "Geez, slow down."

I swing Vivienne around and tuck her against the wall, using my body to shield her from view. Her head tips back, her lips parted and no doubt ready to blast me for manhandling her. I swoop in and snag a kiss before she speaks.

"Vivie," I say pointedly. "I was trying to ask you out."

Her top teeth scrape her bottom lip as she blinks rapidly. "You were?"

Her confusion is adorable. "Yes, I was. I'd like to take you to the Festival of Lights tonight."

She gasps. "Oh my gosh, is Cressida an angel?" *Are you kidding me?*

I move back a step, and Vivienne's hand reaches for my shirt as she rushes to explain. "It's just . . . what she said . . . and that look she gave us," she continues.

"No. No, she's not an angel." I cringe at my too-loud words. The halls are quieter now. No doubt we're going to be late to our classes. "Viv, we can't talk about that kind of stuff here."

Recognition sets in. "Right." She releases me and straightens. "You're right. I'm sorry. My mind is thinking nonstop about everything. I snapped."

Her mind's going nonstop? "I've tried talking with you about everything for days now. You brush me off each time."

"Get to class." A voice of authority rings through the hall.

Vivienne's head snaps toward the voice. "Crap, I can't be late."

Yep, always the rule follower. We rush toward her next class along with the other stragglers.

"Did you not hear me at all?" I ask when the door to AP Calculus comes into view. I peek through the glass and breathe a sigh of relief. No teacher. "I asked you on a date," I remind her.

"You did?" Vivienne's nose scrunches, and her mouth twists in thought. *Way to make a guy feel good, Viv.* "Oh, you did! The Festival of Lights. I'm sorry, I promise I was half listening."

The bell sounds, and Vivienne yelps. Lifting to her toes, she presses a kiss to my cheek and leans closer to my ear. "Of course, I'll go with you."

I remain in the entrance as she hurries inside. Cressida's remark replays. We have to tell Vivienne about the other supernaturals in town. If the nymph picked up on it . . . *oh, shit!* Nymphs distinguish between the mortal and immortal. Vivienne *is* immortal.

"Where's Viv?" Elias asks when I walk into the Ski-Ventures office at the hangar after school.

"I left her at the library. She thinks she's sneaky, but I know she's trying to research the history of the town. She's not a good liar."

Elias steeples his fingers as he leans back in his cracked leather chair. "What does she want to know?"

"What do you think? You told her she's of angel descent. I imagine she's looking for her family history. Or maybe she's trying to figure out what else goes on in this town. A nymph made a telling comment today."

"A nymph? So Phaedra's blood is that strong? It offers Vivienne immortality."

"That's my guess. That's how nymphs work, isn't it? I could ask her what she sees in Viv. Viv suspected Cressida was an angel. We have to tell her about the other species before she asks too many questions."

Too many questions, especially when it comes to the supernatural side of town, can get you killed. Per the underground gossip channels, Roman Bishop's deceased wife, Jenni Ravenal, is a good example of that point.

"If other creatures have picked up on her angel side, then the Court may want to speak with her sooner rather than later."

"I thought you were handling the Court. I don't trust them, Elias. I don't want her dealing with that, if possible. Especially not with Roman."

"They won't hurt her, but she needs to control her powers as they come alive." His phone alarm sounds, and Elias stands. "We also need to speak with Rachel. We need to know who her father is, Breckin. I'm not sure Phaedra's grace can be that strong within Viv. There has to be something more."

Something good, or bad? "Why wouldn't it be strong? Is there something different about Phaedra? We need to know the whole story. *I* need to know the whole story, E. I need to understand about Hamon."

"Look, I have to make a flight. I have a group to pick up on Mount Sousa. The annual Silicon Valley pricks are back."

My father hates humans. Elias hates Silicon Valley humans. It's a group of douche-canoe guys who ski Havenwood Falls this time every year, dropping their tech money around town and hitting on women like they don't already have wives and kids at home. The Court obviously likes their cash or they wouldn't be invited back each year. There are strict rules and memory wards to keep people from remembering their visits to Havenwood Falls.

"Paul gave me stock advice this time," he mutters while I follow him out back to his helicopter.

"Nice guy."

"Well, it's better than the advice I got last year on how to 'have my cake and eat it too.'"

"I'll go out on a limb and assume he wasn't talking about actual cake?" I snort.

"No, he was not." Throwing his ball cap on, Elias stops and looks at me seriously. "You know Viv won't find anything at the library, don't you? Anything chronicling the supernatural events in town is probably kept with the Luna Coven."

"I know. She's being stubborn and pretending everything is normal. I figure I'll let her do her digging."

"Breckin, you need to watch her. I know you want to keep things as normal as possible, but if she changes too much, we'll have to come up with plans. And you're right—we do need to talk about you and your father."

"That's not what I meant." I don't want to discuss me and Hamon. I want to know about Hamon and Elias, and their past with Phaedra.

"I know what you meant, but he needs to tell you those things. He needs to be involved—"

"Soon," I cut him off. I'm not ready to involve Hamon. That means dealing with my birthday and what comes next. "I'm with her almost twenty-four seven. If things change—"

This time he interrupts me. "*When* they change."

He's right. When things change.

We take off at the same time, on different wings. Like a lovesick fool, I left my Bronco at the library in case Vivienne needed a quick escape. She's a horrible driver—her admission, not mine. Hopefully it'll remain in one piece if she takes it for a spin. Thankfully, the vehicle is parked at the street, exactly where I left it, when I return. As I walk up the icy, salted path to the large doors, I look over the building. This is the first time I've bothered to stop by since it was rebuilt after the fire last year that killed Jenni. It's impressive. The Gothic-Victorian design is appealing in a way one might not expect. I smile as I step into the large entryway and am greeted by two carved wooden gargoyles flanking the intricately designed balcony on the second floor. Everett Weston has a sense of humor.

"What's so funny?"

My gaze snaps from the grinning creatures to my grinning Vivienne. She moves with the grace of an angel—head high, steps quiet—and around her is a glow. It's subtle, much like the other day at Coffee Haven, but it's there. I flex my fingers, their need to reach for her deep-seated.

Vivienne halts and runs her hand through her hair, tucking it behind her ear as her grin grows. "That look is dangerous." Her voice is so muted I ask her to repeat herself.

She must be on a mission to kill me, because she closes the ten feet between us and steps into my space. Her chest brushes mine. "I said, that look is dangerous. You remind me of a wild animal looking for a meal."

Divesting her of her backpack, my arm snakes around her waist. "You wouldn't be wrong."

"No?"

I shake my head. "You're glowing, Vivie."

Her lips tremble as her eyes lower to the hands she placed on my chest when I drew her in. She flips her hand over, staring like she doesn't recognize her own appendage. The glow is already fading. "The library is boring alone. I was happy to see you," she says, her eyes meeting mine.

Her words are a balm to my soul. Each time she admits her feelings, I fear my chest will explode. I didn't grow up on feelings. Feelings are a weakness. Even Elias, as semi-normal as he pretends to be, says emotions are complicated. Giving her a squeeze, I breathe in the familiar ginger-and-mint scent she wears like a second skin and reluctantly step back.

"Remind me to show you something later, after the festival," I say as I weave my fingers through hers.

Her gorgeous head angles to the side. "Why later?"

"Because I have something else planned for right now. Are you ready to go?"

"Yep, I was sitting at the window in the other room waiting for you."

~

"You GONNA TELL me what were you smiling about when I found you in the foyer back there?" Vivienne asks once we're settled into my Bronco.

I glance at her sitting beside me. It's not more than thirty degrees outside and her coat is in her lap. Her body doesn't shake from the cold at all. I stretch my arm across the cab and touch her cheeks. They're red from warmth.

"You still haven't told me what you think about all this. About your being part angel," I counter as I start the engine.

"That's because I don't know." She tugs the sleeves of her sweater over her palms, a sign she's not ready to talk. I push anyway.

"What were you looking for in there?" I ask, pulling into the traffic on First Street.

"Looking for?" Her impossibly bad poker face emerges. "I have a paper due. I was doing research for my paper."

"No one goes to the library to do research anymore."

Her brows snap together, offended. "Sure they do. I like it in there. It's so peaceful and the fabrics and furniture—"

"Peaceful, huh?" I take the intersection at First and Main too fast, and my arm swings in front of Vivienne's chest instinctively as we go airborne for two seconds. "It's peaceful because no one uses it," I finish when all four tires are on the ground.

She bursts into laughter. "You just arm-seat-belted me."

"I what?"

Pulling one leg beneath her, she turns in her seat. "You're just like my mom. You threw your arm out to protect me. That's so sweet."

"Why are you talking like that? Stop, it's creepy."

"What? You don't like this?" she asks in a high-pitched baby voice. She might as well run her nails down a chalkboard, that's how appealing it is. She laughs harder. "Oh my gosh. You really *don't* like it. You should see your face; you look like you're going to puke."

Her head falls forward as she clutches her stomach, and I pull the Bronco into a parking spot at the edge of Miller Plaza.

"You think you're funny, don't you?" My grip tightens around the steering wheel.

She giggles. "Poor Breckin. You don't like baby talk?" The pouty face she makes is damn near impossible not to love, but that voice . . .

"Vivie, I swear—" I hiss, breathing through my nose. She mocks me, laughing harder with every word. When she doesn't stop, I reach across the seat and give her a tweak, right above the knee cap.

She jumps in her seat. I tweak it again.

"No." She slaps at my hand with a yelp. *Hello ticklish spot, thy name is karma.* I barely give her a moment to catch her breath from laughing at me before I'm halfway onto her side of the car and attacking her. My hands are everywhere—her knee, her thigh, her side. Her ribs are especially sensitive, and the moment I figure that out, she's a goner.

"Uncle, uncle!" She's scooched so far down in her seat, she's nearly flat on her back with her legs pulled to her chest. Her feet kick at the air. "Breckin!"

Her hands have gone from slapping at mine to protecting herself.

"You done with the baby talk?" I ask firmly, my hands hovering above her.

Her blond hair is a tangled mess around her face, but I get one eyeball—one very narrowed *you are going to die* eyeball—through a part in the silken mess. I wiggle my fingers and move back in. She screams.

"Okay, I promise. No baby talk."

With a satisfied smirk, I offer her my hand and tug until she's sitting again. She huffs and straightens her twisted sweater. Blue eyes flick my way, a little side glance, and I catch her lips twitching with suppressed humor as she shoves her hair from her face.

Emotions swell within, and I grab her face and plant my lips on hers. Hard. My fingers curve around the base of her skull, sinking into her hair while my mouth parts hers for one satisfying, but fast, taste. I pull away as quickly as I attacked, so quickly that Vivienne's hands don't have time to make it past grabbing my forearms for support.

Thoughts spill from my mind. "I can't lose you."

Vivienne draws a sharp breath.

"I won't." I shake my head and touch our foreheads. "It would kill me, Vivie."

Her hands slip to cup my jaw. "You won't lose me," she says tenderly.

"You don't understand. I'm not willing to give this up. This laughter, this light. I didn't know what I was missing until my soul found yours." I close my eyes. God, that is so cliché. So trite, but how else do I convey the difference having her makes?

"Breckin, I get it. I do." Her hands apply the barest pressure to my skin, and I open my eyes and meet her gaze. "I grew up loved by a mother and friends. I didn't hide the way you have, but I think I understand what you're saying. Every time I see you, this bond grows stronger. That glowing I keep doing is all for you, obviously."

"Obviously," I mock playfully.

Her smile could sustain me for months. Our lips touch with a feather-soft brush before she looks past me. "What are we doing here?"

I release her reluctantly and move back behind the wheel of the Bronco. "Right. I'd kind of forgotten I drove here." We're in the shopping plaza across from the high school and medical center. "I figured we could get dinner for your mom."

Vivienne looks at the strip center and where we're parked. "Dinner from Sakura?"

"Oh boy. Your face is melting. Don't you dare get all mushy on me again."

"Whatever." She bends over and digs her cell from her bag on the floorboard. "I'll message Mom. She loves the moo goo gai pan from here. I can't believe you thought of her. How did you know I was supposed to bring her dinner tonight?"

I lift my brows.

"Right," she nods, "super angel hearing. You overheard me talking to her this morning before school, didn't you?"

"I might have," I admit. Vivienne bites her lip as her hands go to work, typing on her phone. I chuckle. "And because I see you slowly dying inside, yes, I did hear what she said about me, too."

"Ugh. You did?" Her butt slides forward as she cowers in her seat. "She's so embarrassing."

"She's not embarrassing. She's smart." With that, I grab my keys and jump out of the car. I feel Vivienne's eyes roll as I walk around the Bronco and open her door for her.

"You did hear the part where she warned me about boys like you?" she asks as she drops her legs out the door and hops down. "Is that why you're saying she's smart?"

"I heard the part where she said you were lucky to have caught a gorgeous specimen such as myself."

She pokes my ribs and laughs. "Yeah, I think what she actually said was that Breckin seems like he's the kind of guy who would have a massive ego. Are you positive you want to date a guy like that?"

The real conversation was more about how her mom worried Vivienne was cutting out Zara—who's driven her to and from school for years—for me. Her mother promised Vivienne that she did like me, and she admitted I was too charming and handsome for my own good—a smart observation. Then she warned her daughter of the pitfalls of going out with guys who could date whomever they wanted, and told her to not forget her morals or future.

"And what was your reply?" I ask with a grin.

"I said you would do, for now." She flips her hair over her shoulder haughtily and brushes by me.

I snag her from behind, my lips grazing the curve of her ear. "For now?"

Vivienne reaches up and grabs the back of my head, holding me so we're cheek to cheek. "Forever," she says, turning and pressing her lips to the edge of my mouth.

Snap. "Shit," I mutter.

Vivienne's head turns farther, her eyes going wide. "You seem to be having a hard time controlling those things."

"What makes you say that?" I shake my wings out, irritated to no end at their willfulness. The moment the itch hit my spine, I cloaked them. Thankfully, it's dark outside and the parking lot is poorly lit. Anyone watching us will have no idea I just ripped another shirt and flashed them with my wings.

"I thought I learned how to control this when I was twelve. See what you do to me?"

I return to the truck, willing my wings back in place as I reach for my leather jacket in the back seat.

"Mom replied she'd love to see us for dinner," Vivienne tells me through her laughter.

"Perfect. I'm starving."

"Hey," she says, taking my hand as I return to her side. "Afterwards, let's skip the festival and just stay in."

Stay in? This girl dragged me all over town for the Hot Cocoa & Cookie Crawl. She's repeatedly told me how much she loves doing town events—movie nights, festivals, art events—and now she wants to stay in?

"Is my surly attitude rubbing off on you?" I tease, running my thumb over the back of her hand as we head toward Sakura.

She bites her lip and turns her head. "Can't a girl just want a quiet night in?"

I tug on her hand, stopping her progress mid–parking lot. "You can want whatever you want, Vivie. I just want to make sure you're not saying no because you're scared of something, or because you think I don't want to go."

"What if it's a little of all three?" she asks. I cock my head, and she continues, "I know you don't love these events, I'm afraid the crowds draw more fallen who might be looking for us to the area, and I want to be alone with you."

"Tell you what, let's bring your mom dinner and see how we feel afterward. Okay?"

She agrees with a small smile, but there's an uncertainty in her eyes that wasn't there before she learned about her lineage. Another worry to add to her collection. I long to remove all her worries.

DON'T LET ME GO

VIVIENNE

*H*avenwood Falls Medical Center is my second home. Or third, considering I spent much of my time at Zara's when we were younger and Mom needed a sitter. Breckin and I enter through the break room door at the back of the converted house and unpack our take-out.

"So this is a hospital?" Breckin asks as he looks around the room.

"More like emergency clinic. If anyone is seriously injured, Elias life-flights them to a higher-level trauma center. Usually Denver or Colorado Springs, I think." I dig through the cabinets and pull three canned drinks from Mom's stash. "I would have thought you knew that."

Breckin waves off the soda. "I did know that, but I've never been in here. Or any doctor's office." He draws a halo over his head and grins.

My hands go to my hips. "Whoa, wait a minute. Are you telling me I didn't need all those shots through the years?" I ask. Breckin shrugs a shoulder. "Not fair." I pout.

"What's not fair?" Mom asks as she walks into the break room. "Hi, sweetie." Her hand smooths the hair back from my face the same way she did when I was five. She looks at Breckin.

"Breckin, good to see you again."

46

"Ms. Freeman." Breckin clasps his hands in front of him. The boy deals with angels, fought a reaper, and flies like a rocket through the sky, but my mother makes him nervous.

"Ah, Sakura—massive bonus points for this." Mom's face lights up as she takes a seat in one of the plastic chairs and motions for us to follow. "So, what's not fair?" she repeats.

"Oh, nothing important. I was just talking about something that happened at school."

"What have you two been up to this afternoon?" she asks between bites of snap peas and mushrooms. My gaze flicks to Breckin, then back. Mom's brow furrows. "Viv? You didn't go running, did you? I don't want you out there alone."

Breckin grunts his little over-my-dead-body grunt. It's been one month. Should I know the meanings of all his sounds already? "Don't worry. She won't be running alone anymore."

I turn on my boyfriend as Mom's eyes pop wide. "Excuse me?" I ask, taken back by his firm refusal.

He flashes an innocent smile, and I swear he turns up his angel glow. Is he trying to manipulate me by using his abilities? Dropping my spork in my chicken fried rice, I prop my chin on my fist and give him a stare down. My mother watches our interaction with a smile.

"Viv, we've talked about this," Breckin says meaningfully.

"Oh, I know what we've talked about. I'm just surprised you're sitting here in front of my mother, telling her what I will and won't do, like you have a say."

Mom purses her lips, and I expect her to butt in. Having a single mom growing up taught me one important lesson—don't take crap from guys. She won't scold my attitude if I'm sticking up for myself.

Breckin doesn't squirm. Not even an inch. "You don't think I know better than to tell you what to do?" His amber gaze focuses on my mother, and he graces her with another grin. "You raised a stubborn daughter."

"Don't I know it," Mom says pointedly. "I've never liked her running alone, so we have something we can agree on."

"Are you two ganging up on me now? Mom, I told you I wasn't

comfortable running anymore." She may not know about the attack that left me for dead, but everyone in town knows about Heidi Bennett's disappearance. It's been an easy excuse to use when Zara or Mom ask me why I stopped running. "And for the record, Breckin, if I want to run, you won't stop me."

"See, this is where you've read me all wrong, Viv. I would never try to stop you from doing anything you want to do. I'll just follow at your side."

"Like a stalker?"

"No, like a caring boyfriend who doesn't want anything to happen to you."

"You hate running," I remind him needlessly. *Why run when you can fly?*

"Not as much as I hate thinking of you getting hurt." *Again.* I hear the last word in my head, but whether he said it or it's implied, I can't be sure. My mind goes to the scene in the car earlier. *I can't lose you.*

His actions and words are a testament to the way he loves me. That one sentence is all that's needed to douse my irritation with him. If we were alone, I'd pull him close and . . .

"This is a non-issue, anyway," I tell them before my imagination gets carried away. "Like I've said, more than once, I don't plan on running outside anymore. Plus, my cross-country career is over."

"If it's a non-issue, why are you arguing with us?" he asks.

I toss a fortune cookie at Breckin's gorgeous head as Mom dissolves into laughter.

Crossing my arms over my chest, I slouch in my chair. "We brought you dessert for a midnight snack, but I'm not sure I want to give it to you anymore."

Breckin chokes on his own laughter. "She probably won't want it. How good can flan from an Asian restaurant be?"

"How good can—" Mom's mouth drops. "Have you never had the flan from Sakura?"

His top lip curls in disgust.

"Breckin isn't big on sweets. He ridicules everything I love as being too sugary," I explain while cleaning up my dinner trash. Mom's gasp fills the break room. The Freeman girls are known around town for their love of desserts. We're famous at the annual dessert crawl.

He shrugs. "Sorry, Viv's as sweet as I get."

My face heats up, and Breckin reaches across the table and touches my hand.

Mom has always known how to read me, but right now she's reading us, and her look speaks volumes. A dark shadow crosses her face before she shakes it off and smiles. "All right, that's enough sappy sugar out of you two. I need to get back to work."

WE FORGO THE FESTIVAL, return to my apartment, and work on homework with the television on in the background until ten, the official time Mom has ruled as Breckin's curfew at our place when she's not home.

What she doesn't know is that my boyfriend can fly. So, although he leaves at ten, it's only for the twenty minutes it takes him to drive his Bronco home, then return using his wings. I use that time to shower and get ready for bed, but I'm not fast enough, and Breckin is sprawled face down on my bed when I finish, his dark wings spread wide. The iridescent coloring shimmers beneath my ceiling fan light as they twitch and tremble about. Knowing how sensitive they are, I carefully brush my fingers along the edge.

Breckin heaves a euphoric sigh and turns his head on my pillow. "I've hidden them more since you've been in my life than ever before. They're dying to stretch out."

I love the sleek quality his feathers have. They're downy soft around his spine and along the underside, but the rest are like smooth ebony silk with amber-tipped edges.

"Well, I won't tell them no." I tease my fingertips over the feathers. Not even the promise of Breckin's shirtless skin can tear my gaze away from studying him. I chew on my lip thoughtfully. "Do you think I might get wings?"

His flutter, and I grin. "You like that idea, huh?"

Breckin pushes his chest from the bed, inches over and lifts his left wing. He pats the space beside him, and I crawl onto my stomach at his side. Once I'm settled, his wing lowers over me like a blanket. Its weight is heavier than I expected. I love it.

I rest my cheek on my folded hands and study his face while he tangles his fingers into the wet ends of my hair. "I'm not sure if I could physically handle seeing you with wings, Vivie."

My heart pumps a little harder and a little faster than before. The idea of having wings is both terrifying and intriguing. How will I cope with the changes as they come? At what point will I become less human and more angel? Or will I ever?

"Hey." He tugs my bottom lip down with the tip of his pinky. "Remember I said I wanted to show you something today at the library?"

My cheek rubs the back of my hand as I nod.

"Close your eyes."

I do as he asks, but can't help but laugh. "You want to show me something, but I have to close my eyes?"

"Mmmhmmm."

The sight of the back of my eyelids slowly changes from black to red, and my fingers shield my eyes automatically. "Breckin? What are you doing?"

My mattress moves under his weight as he shifts next to me. "Open your eyes and find out."

I crack one eye, then slam it shut. "Holy . . . what is that?"

All I saw was bright white through my fingers and cracked lid.

Breckin snickers. "Okay, open them again."

This time I'm greeted with a glowing white, but it's not blinding, like before. I blink a few times, getting used to the extra light, and push to my knees. The glow is Breckin. He's tucked his wings close to his back and rolled to his side, giving me the perfect view of his ripped abs, angel muscles, and celestial glow.

I'm in awe. "When you said I glowed, this is what you meant? What Zara saw?"

"No, your glow isn't half as bright as this." My face falls, and he laughs. "Don't be jealous. I've been an angel a lot longer than you have, you overachiever."

I'm drawn to him. My hands reach forward like they're beyond my control. I'm a marionette, and someone else holds the strings. His skin doesn't feel any different. It's warm, like always. The muscles, more defined than normal seventeen-year-old boys', jump and bunch at my touch, and Breckin sucks in air through his teeth.

His hand covers mine. "Do you feel the pull?" he asks through gritted teeth.

"To touch you?" I ask breathlessly, wetting my lips.

"That's the angel pull, Viv. My glow speaks to that part of you. Whenever you're around another angel who shines their light, you'll feel a closeness to them, but I think our soul mate bond makes ours more powerful."

The brightness fades slowly, and I smile, my mind forming the mental picture of him on a dimmer switch. I shake the random thought away. "Why do you think our bond makes it different?"

"I've been around other angels when they let their grace shine. Other girl angels," he says with an incline of his head to make sure I understand what he's saying. "It didn't affect me at all, but with you, I have a horrible time keeping my hands off you when you start glowing. It makes me feel possessive, and I'm gonna be honest—it makes me have thoughts I shouldn't be having."

"Breckin." I shove at his chest, but he doesn't budge.

"I'm just saying. It's, um . . . very tempting." He explains needlessly. My body still hums with the need to get close to him. Temptation is certainly a thing between us. "I showed you that because I imagine you will be a full-blown light bulb sooner or later, and we need to get it under control. When I saw you at the library this afternoon, it hit me. We can't let you evolve without help."

Evolve? Funny word for an angel to use. "What does that mean?"

"That means you are about to embark on angel training."

"Angel training?"

"Yep." He reaches for my arms and drags me back down to his side. "It's time we both get in shape for the things to come, Vivie."

He speaks with excitement, but my body registers the way he squeezes a little tighter. His birthday is four months away. Even if I'm in the clear since Sebastian is dead, and hopefully no one knows, or cares, about my existence and our bond—we still have Hamon to deal with.

HOLY GROUND

BRECKIN

*A*ngel training sucks.

Vivienne and I head to Elias's hangar every day after school and on Saturday and Sunday, to work on whatever he deems necessary. Most days, he separates us, sending me to lift weights or run while he works with her in private.

"Breckin, you distract her," he snaps when I complain about being sent away.

"I do not. I just want to help her. She said she's having a hard time finding that switch within. Maybe I can show her—"

"No." He's already turning his back to leave me behind.

"What is your problem?" I shout across the hangar. My voice echoes in the empty space. Elias looks over his shoulder, his icy blue eyes staring me down. "You know what, forget it. Do it your way. I'll go lift more weights, because that's going to help."

"WHAT'S GOING on with you and Elias?" Vivienne asks after a few weeks at the hangar. "Why are you so angry with him?"

It's Friday night, and we're sitting by the firepit on my back patio. January has remained uneventful. We go to school and we go to the hangar, and we try to keep up with our classwork, too. When her mother doesn't work, Vivienne spends time with her, and I train with Elias on fighting. Honing skills that come naturally.

I poke at the burning wood, causing embers to fly. "I'm not angry with him."

Her knee knocks mine. "And you call me a terrible liar."

"What do you two do while he has me working out?" I ask. They haven't told me. Three and a half weeks of seeing him almost daily, and neither of them have said a word to me about what they talk about or work on up in his apartment. She's supposed to be learning how to control any abilities that come to life, but she still glows when I walk into a room after an extended time apart. "Why is it a secret? From me, of all people, Vivie."

Vivienne pushes up out of her Adirondack chair and stands in front of me, kicking at my legs. I angle sideways and she slips into my lap, her tiny frame resting perfectly against my chest.

"I wouldn't keep secrets from you." She touches my cheek.

"Then what—" I don't finish as a vision scratches across my mind. It's fleeting—a scene of Elias's stern face, his lips moving, but I can't hear his words—then it's gone, the scene sucked back like a black hole swallowed it.

I nearly toss Vivienne from my lap. "Was that you?" Her tired smile confirms it. "He's teaching you mental manipulation?"

"Sort of. He's been trying to teach me how to access my gifts, but all I seem good at is projecting thoughts or visions."

I use manipulation often. It's an easy fix for when humans stumble upon me accidentally being too nonhuman. I just touch them and give them something else to think about. It's a good power for her to have access to.

"You're not missing out on anything. I sit on his couch and meditate for hours on end, trying to find my angel side," she says as she leans back and meets my eyes. "Most of the time I get nothing but a horrible headache. Showing you that little bit wiped me out."

The resonant rumbling of a motorcycle fills the night, and Vivienne snuggles closer, a small groan leaving her lips.

"What's wrong?"

"They freak me out."

"They?" I lean to the side and peer down the road. A solitary headlight shines in the distance. Although it's built above ground level on a wall, the side patio to my house is open to the street. Our wrought-iron fencing provides security, but not privacy. There's no need for privacy when I can cloak myself if I don't want to be seen.

"Those motorcycle guys," she clarifies.

I tighten my arms and laugh. "Vivie, it's a motorcycle club, and they're not going to bother you."

"They're a gang! Swords of the Infernal Night—S.I.N.—that can't be good."

"And you're an angel who will kick ass with the best of us soon," I remind her, brushing her hair with a kiss. She scoffs as though I've overestimated her future abilities. "It's only one bike, anyway. Stop fretting."

The biker moves in graceful slow motion as he nears the intersection of Fairchild and Eleventh. He plants his feet, shifting on his bike seat while his head swings toward us. Jack Peters. He idles through the intersection and stops even with us. Vivienne's fingers clutch at my shirt until the fabric is taut across my stomach.

"Peters?" Jack's not one to stop and speak. Ever. He nods a silent greeting, and his head tips from side to side. My gaze flicks to Vivienne in my lap. *Shit.* Gripping her hips, I push her to her feet and stand behind her. "Something going on?" I ask cryptically.

"What is she?" he asks, his voice deep for a seventeen-year-old.

I rub her lower back, willing her to remain calm. "Part angel, and that's not yet public knowledge."

He shakes his dark head. "There's something else there, Breckin." He turns back to the road. "By the way, there are fallen ones hanging around. And damned," he adds before he pulls his feet from the asphalt and takes off. The rumbling from his engine bounces between the houses.

Vivienne spins in my arms, bumping into my chest in her haste. "What was that, Breckin? He knew what I was? Wasn't that Jack

Peters? I've never seen him talk to anyone. I've seen him stop by the firehouse when his dad is working and I'm at Napoli's, but that's it. How in the hell does he know I'm anything other than human?"

Her questions come at me in rapid succession.

"Viv, take a breath." My gaze roams the sky. *There are damned hanging around.* I fight the urge to hide her inside.

"Take a breath? Jack Peters knows what I am," she spits out each word. "He mentioned the fallen. Does he mean your dad? More reapers?"

"No. Reapers aren't fallen, remember?" My angel side knocks at my back to be let out, paranoid about what could be watching us.

"What did he mean by damned?" her voice shakes.

Have I not explained angels to her better than this? "There are angels on earth who work for Heaven—they carry out the Creator's divine plans. Then there are the fallen, the ones who were either cast out or defected, and those who left but don't align specifically with either side. In that sense, Elias is considered fallen. And last, there are the damned. They are the ones who aligned with Hell." Hamon is a bit between fallen and damned. He lures humans into sin, which is to Hell's benefit. I always assumed he'd aligned with Hell, but Elias says Hamon is more of an independent contractor. An angel angry with God and mankind for reasons I've never been made to understand.

Her eyes grow wide with my explanation. "And how does he know about me?"

"Jack's not human, Viv." I take her hand and lead her to the back door.

She tugs back. "He's angel, too?"

I exert a bit more force on her hand, and she follows again. "He's not."

"Not an angel. So, he's something else." We step inside, and I lock the door, draw the shades, and turn to find Vivienne with her arms crossed, her hip popped, and her face screwed up. She means business. "What is he?"

"He is a hellhound. They have excellent senses, especially when it comes to angels and demons. Or the dead." She sways slightly on her feet, and I take her by the shoulders. "Viv, I wanted to fill you in sooner, but Elias wanted you to establish control of your abilities first."

"Fill me in on what?"

"Angels are not the only supernatural beings in Havenwood Falls. There are more. A lot more."

I settle Vivienne on the couch in the basement and go to the kitchen to make her a hot chocolate. While the milk warms, I send Elias a text letting him know about Jack's comment. There are other angels in Havenwood Falls, but Jack specified the damned. He meant the ones we'd want to be on watch for. They might be hanging around and keeping an eye on me for Hamon. Or they could be passing by innocently. There's also the off chance they're looking for Vivienne. The options are numerous, and I'm not taking any chances.

Vivienne's lying on the couch, her head resting against the back cushion, when I lean over the back with a large mug in hand. "Extra chocolate, extra marshmallows."

A wobbly smile greets me when she tips her chin up. "You know me well."

Taking a seat on the end, I pick up her feet and put them in my lap. "So, I'm gonna go out on a limb and assume you have questions."

Her blond brows lift. "You think?"

Where do I begin? This town was founded on the idea that supernaturals and humans could live together peacefully. There are wards and rules, but for many species, this place is the closest thing to living freely they will ever find.

"Ask me whatever you want, and I'll answer truthfully," I say when I can't come up with the right opening.

She blows across the top of her mug. "You say supernatural and I think unicorns."

"You're such a girl, Vivie."

"No unicorns then?" Her smile is disarming. It's the smile of a fragile girl who has no idea what she is about to learn exists in the world.

"There are a lot of shifters here. Wolves, mountain lions, bears, dragons, and yes, unicorns."

The mug lowers from her mouth. "You're not kidding, are you? Shifters? Like people who change into animals? They change into dragons?" Her eyes grow wider with each question she asks.

"They do." The library comes to mind. "Remember my smile at the library?" She inclines her head slightly as she takes a sip of her drink. "There were carved gargoyles decorating the foyer. Everett Weston designed the place. He is a gargoyle."

Vivienne chokes, a dribble of chocolate dripping from her lip. "A stone statue? That hot man is a—"

My jaw scissors as she catches what she's said. "Hot man, huh?" I ask, and Vivienne's mouth opens and closes twice as I explain Everett. "Obviously, he isn't a stone creature. A gargoyle is a protector. Everett is part of the Spiritual Assembly of Protectors, which means he can take on divine assignments. That is the only reason I give you his name specifically. We would consider him an ally if we needed one."

"Meaning there are gargoyles that are not allies?"

"Vivie, there is good and evil in everyone, human or otherwise."

"This is so insane," she mutters, and I agree.

This is insane. Humans hide in a bubble, thinking they're the only intelligent species on earth. That good and evil is as simple as black and white. That they are the ones who make the rules, when in truth many of the residents in this town could destroy everything with little more than a snap of their fingers, or a shot of fire from their lungs.

"I'm not sure how much trouble I could get in for telling you this."

"Trouble from whom?"

"The Court of the Sun and the Moon."

"The Court—" Vivienne leans over and puts her mug on the coffee table. "You should probably start at the beginning."

Explaining everything I know takes time. The Court, the wards, the creatures. I stay away from naming names, although she asks, preferring to stick to the basics.

"Elias has worked with the Court several times when there were issues with angels in the area. Because of that, he's been able to keep them from digging into your origins further."

"But I'll have to meet with them eventually?" She chews on the edge of her nail when I nod. "And the magical tattoo thing?"

"That won't be an issue for you. The Court uses the tattoos as a way of registering and keeping track of supernaturals. As angels, we're exempt."

"Why are angels exempt?"

"We're superior. There's nothing the Court can offer us. With vampires, the tattoos allow them to walk in the daylight; with shifters, apparently the tattoo keeps them safe from each other when hunting, among other things. I don't know all the specifics, but those are the basics. Angels are born with more power and abilities than they can offer."

"How have I lived in a town my entire life and never noticed vampires or nymphs? How does no one know?"

"You and half the population. That's the whole point. That's why there are wards to keep the town hidden, and memory spells."

"What about when Sebastian grabbed me at the school? How was his presence covered up?"

"Elias. He went by the school while you were recovering and made sure no one remembered a thing."

The night goes on like this. Vivienne asks questions, and I answer them as best I can.

"I assume you and Elias aren't the only angels here?" I give her foot a squeeze. "Well, you, Elias, and me."

"They come and go, but yes, there are others. Most don't live here like we do. They're here to fulfill a purpose, like guardian angels. There is one, Cecelia—"

"From the music store?" Vivienne's hand goes to her chest. "She's an angel? I should have known. She looks like you would picture an angel to be."

"Vivie, *you* look exactly like what an angel should look like." My palm rubs up her shin. "I still can't figure out how we didn't connect before I healed you. I can't imagine how I never fell for you before."

Vivienne shifts and climbs onto my lap. "For the record, you are way hotter than that gargoyle."

"Yeah?" I grip her hips, reveling in the feel of her weight.

Our lips connect with a light brush as she smiles. "Totally."

"I should get you home," I murmur, glancing at the time, but Vivienne has other ideas.

"I think I should stay for a while," she says, drawing my bottom lip into her mouth and sucking lightly as her hands tangle in my hair, holding me in place.

I dive into her mouth, and her taste is my undoing.

BRAVE

VIVIENNE

*H*avenwood Falls High is a zoo for the supernatural. I still struggle with accessing my angelic side, but my nose no longer struggles with identifying the many creatures I've lived among my entire life. The Kasuns are wolves. They were the first people I unequivocally identified. It happened out of the blue. I walked into the cafeteria for lunch one day, my gaze fell on Kase Kasun and his crew, and *bam,* I just knew. I nearly dropped my soft drink in my haste to get away. Now whenever Breckin and I see Willa, Kase, or one of their pack members, Breckin makes absurd comments about throwing things, just to see if they'll play fetch. It's his way of calming me around the shifters, because my mind can't help but envision my attack last December. I'd assumed it to be a random animal, but Breckin's revelations have brought to light other possibilities. Elias says the sheriff—also a wolf—swears he checked around, and no shifters were to blame. At least now, with my super senses, I'll know when something comes at me.

~

I'm late. Convincing Elias and Breckin to give me a day with Zara was no easy feat. I search for Breckin as I jog across Eighth and hurry down Main toward Callie's Consignments, certain he's lingering nearby. The sun is on full display today, warming the temperature to above normal for late February.

Callie's is huge. Elegant furnishings are strategically placed throughout the store with antique décor complementing the settings. Much of the first floor is filled with clothing and accessories. Most of the items are vintage, which is why my British-obsessed best friend loves the place. Taking a quick glance around, I don't spot Zara.

"Z?" I raise my voice slightly.

"Pretty complexion and dark hair?" I spin at the heavily accented voice, chills dancing up my spine.

"I'm sorry?" I ask, as a dark-haired woman appears from behind the large armoire near the far wall with pillows in hand. She's beautifully exotic, and a bit of a mess with her long dark wind-blown hair and casual plaid shirt over tight jeans. I've never seen her, but something about her has my skin jumping. She's not human, that's for sure.

"Your friend, the one with the dismal British accent?" she asks. Biting my lip at the woman's grimace, I nod. *That's Zara all right.* "She's in the dressing area."

The unease the stranger awoke settles when I move out of her eyeline and step into the dressing area. It's like a gypsy caravan in here. Rich, colorful fabrics cover the walls. Thick carpets are layered on the floor. I'm jealous of the luxury displayed every time I come in here. And it changes constantly. Callie excels at finding unique pieces. If only Mom and I could afford it.

"Z?"

"I wonder if I can find something that says Jane Austen meets Titanic?" Zara ponders through the thick dressing room curtains, ignoring any type of polite greeting. "You know, lace and bead work. Not too frumpy, though."

I take a seat on the vintage couch and sift through the stack of clothing draped over the armrest. "Are these all your things?"

I may be late, but she obviously began her shopping expedition early.

Zara's head pokes out. "Callie really needs trolleys in here. I could barely hold all of that."

"Trolley? You've been reading more slang dictionaries, haven't you?"

"Perhaps." She winks and parts the curtains dramatically. "Take a look at this? Opinion?"

"Opinion? Gorgeous. I love the empire waist and the fabric gathering around the neckline and sleeves." She looks like she stepped out of Regency London.

She does a little twirl in front of the huge gilded mirror leaning against the wall.

"I swear Callie has someone in London to find these things just for me. Even the peacock-blue color is my favorite." When she's done admiring herself, her gaze finds me. "Did you meet Nikita?"

"Who? Oh, you mean the girl out there? Kinda, I guess."

Zara smooths her hands along the skirt of her dress and turns from side to side. "She's Callie's cousin. From New York. Gorgeous, isn't she? She's visiting."

"And you found this all out how?" I ask, impressed with her investigative skills. Maybe I should ask her to look into the history of Havenwood Falls for me.

"I asked her, silly. Callie was walking out when I came in. Nikita—killer name, isn't it?—offered to watch the store for a few minutes. She has this dark, bad-girl vibe to her. I'm totally intrigued."

"You? Miss Jane Austen wannabe, crumpets and lace lover, finds the hot rocker chick intriguing?"

"You know I find anyone new to Havenwood Falls interesting. How often do we get fresh blood here?" Her laugh fills the dressing area. "Anyway, did you not find anything to try on?"

"Prom isn't until May, Z." And though Breckin asked about it, I can't seem to muster up the enthusiasm for it. Our future is so unknown. "I'm not shopping until I have a date." I'm not sure why I lie to her.

Her dark eyes roll. "Um, you planning on breaking up with Breckin between now and May nineteenth?"

"Of course not, but . . ." But his eighteenth birthday is in April, and I still don't know what that means. Will I have my soul mate come May or will I be a complete and utter mess? "I'm just waiting, okay?"

Zara ducks back behind the curtains and proceeds to model four other dresses of similar styles before she moves on to the casual clothing stacked by my hip. I take snapshots on my phone so she can get the "social media view" before making decisions about everything. She's not a diva, but the girl is serious about her clothing. She wants to be a buyer for a fashion line in L.A. or New York. Now that I know there are memory wards on the town, I wonder if she'll ever return to Havenwood Falls once she leaves.

Nikita is nowhere to be seen when we're ready to check out, and my intense feelings are gone.

~

AFTER DUMPING Zara's purchases in her car, we walk to Napoli's for a late lunch. It's a little after two, and the square is bustling. Residents tend to come out of the woodwork when the sun shines in the middle of the winter. Especially after the dreary weather we had this past week. We're nearing the fountain when a fire ignites up my spine, and a groan escapes my lips.

"Viv?"

I stop walking, and my arm reaches behind my back, straining to scratch an itch that isn't an itch. As quickly as it came, the sensation disappears. Zara's brows drop low over her eyes.

"Sorry, I was attacked by an itch." I feign scratching as we continue.

"So, anyway, I was closing last night and guess who came in after his shift at Shelf Indulgence and totally flirted with me?"

I trip over my feet as another pain rends through my back. *What in the ever living hel—lo, angel at five o'clock.*

Propped against a tree, just off the path through the square, is a tall, dark, and uncharacteristically handsome guy a few years older than us.

Behind him are a set of wings that remind me more of a crow than an angel. Almost flat at the top, where Breckin's are rounded, they form the letter T with his body. From tip to tip, the span probably matches his well over six-foot height. The feathers are long and cream with brown specks. They're not beautiful at all, nothing like the inky iridescence of Breckin's.

My back hums with the stir of a thousand nails prodding my skin at once as my gaze roams up his dark chest and our gazes lock. His fiery, reddish-brown orbs study me as I study him, and my heartbeat picks up. Somewhere, in the back of my awakening dread, I hear Zara saying my name. Does no one notice the shirtless angel in their presence? I tear my eyes from his and look around.

"Viv? I swear, where are you today? You've been—"

"Well, well, what do we have here? A baby angel all alone?" I whirl around at the accented voice behind me. "What is your name, precious?"

"—barely paying attention to me all day." Zara drones on, seemingly unaware of the angel before us.

He's cloaked.

The angel turns his head thoughtfully, and the riot of short dreadlocks covering his head flop haphazardly. "Do you want me to show myself for your friend?"

Turning, I thrust one arm through Zara's and reach for the cell phone in my pocket. "C'mon, Z. I thought I saw someone."

We take two steps before a growl sends chills through my body, and I'm jerked back. The cell I'd just fingered flies from my hand to the ground.

"Didn't anyone tell you to never walk away from your superiors, precious?" His grip on my bicep is crippling.

"Hey, let my friend go! Who are you?" Zara rushes forward, her fingers trying to pry his hand away, to no avail. The angel grips her wrist, his lips moving slightly before he shoves her.

"What did you do?" I ask him frantically, as Zara walks away.

"I thought we could use some alone time." He smiles. Then there's a flash, and two seconds later, I'm falling to my knees and rolling on the ground. We're in the alley between the buildings around the square, but we moved so fast, I didn't even feel it.

"What are you?" He sniffs as I scramble back. My knees sting, and I look down at my torn pants, blood coloring the fabric.

Wiping the debris from my torn-up palms, I gain my footing. "Who are you?"

"I am Zeke, my little half-breed." He pushes closer, knocking me into the brick wall at my back. "Who created you?"

"I don't know."

"You don't know?" Zeke laughs. His hand touches my throat, the sharp tip of his nail scratching my skin as he draws it down along my veins, outlining the V of my shirt. "I think I'll take you with me and see what we can find out about you." His face moves closer, and I tense as his tongue touches my cheek. "I'd like a taste of this pretty skin."

Ignoring the wet scrape of his tongue along my skin, I draw a deep breath, then jerk to the side while coming around and grabbing Zeke's head from behind. Using all my strength, I slam his face into the wall, then I take off at a sprint. His growl ignites my terror, but I don't dare scream. What if a human saw us? I don't want anyone to get hurt because of me. Where did Zara go?

I bounce off Zeke's chest. Shuffling back, I turn and run the other way. In a blink, he's before me again. He's transporting. I can't get away.

"I'm nobody. I didn't even know I had angel blood." I snap my jaw shut. *Stupid Viv.*

His orange eyes light up. "You're the girl," he says. "The soul mate."

My vision blurs, then clears. I have nowhere to go and no real power over this strong creature, but I'll fight to keep myself and Breckin safe. I allow him to close the distance between us, then kick at his thigh. The bone in my shin cracks, and I drop to the ground.

"You are weak." Zeke stands over me. "We can make you strong. You and your soul mate. Think of everything you could have."

"I don't know what you're talking about." Pain shoots along my leg, burning with a fire that should have me writhing. When Sebastian attacked me, I could barely speak from the pain.

"You think we don't know who you belong to, beautiful?" His booted foot steps on my thigh, and I wince. "We have plans for you and your little Nephilim."

He cracks a dark smile, then stomps his leg down on mine. His heavy boot snaps my femur, and each fracture and splinter within the bone grates in my ears. My scream could wake the dead.

Zeke laughs and licks his lips. He looks at me like I'm his favorite dessert, and my stomach roils. It is his lust that holds his attention when another angel appears in a blink behind him with a blinding sword and punishment written on his familiar face.

The blade slices Zeke's head clean off before he knows what's hit him. I push backward as Zeke's body disintegrates into nothing but embers falling onto my body. Heat stings my cheek, and I swipe the ash away, feeling ill.

I look up at the avenging angel who swooped in to save me. He doesn't look happy. "You should be healing. Can't you heal?"

My head answers with a slight shake from side to side when my voice refuses to speak. The sword disappears, then he's on his haunches sliding his arms beneath my knees. I bite my lip, tasting blood, as I try to keep from screaming. My vision blurs.

"Put your arms around my neck and hang on."

I comply, locking my fingers around his neck and trying not to press too close to his skin. My gaze focuses on his large wings. Up close like this, they're varying shades of grey outlined in white. Like someone took a white marker and traced the edges of each and every feather. They snap out, and we shoot into the air. Unlike Zeke, who seemed to transport us from one spot to the other, we fly. But we fly at a speed Breckin has never dared, and we arrive at Breckin's house before the contents of my stomach can evacuate via my mouth.

My limbs shake as he stalks toward the glass doors that open to Breckin's back patio. *Where is my angel?* No sooner do I have the thought than an agonizing scream reaches inside my head.

A growl I recognize as Breckin's fills the backyard. He lands at full speed, his feet hitting the deck and skidding as his wings stir up the snow.

"What did you do to her?" Breckin runs for me, his face twisted with pain. "Vivie? I'm sorry . . . I should have been there. Are you all right?" His hands reach for me. "Give her to me," he orders boldly.

The arms holding me tighten. "Open the door, and we can lay her inside."

Heat rushes from the house when Breckin opens the glass door. He slaps his arm across the threshold, blocking our entrance. "If you did this, I will kill you. Father or not."

Hamon doesn't respond, and Breckin drops his arm, so we can pass. Hamon's arms shift beneath my legs as he turns sideways to fit me through the door. The small amount of jostling makes my leg explode with pain once again. Tears overflow.

Breckin winces as his hand goes to his temple.

"What's wrong?" I ask through gritted teeth.

Breckin smooths his face somewhat. He can't hide the creases around his tight lips and narrowed eyes. He's in pain. My gaze remains pinned on him as he follows closely behind Hamon, pointing us toward the same bedroom I woke up in the last time an angel tossed me around.

"She's not healing. You need to heal her," Hamon says brusquely as he sets me carefully upon the guest bed.

"Of course I'm going to heal her." Breckin pushes by his father. His hands go right to my leg, ripping my jeans from ankle to thigh. He lowers his face to mine, kissing my lips as his hands graze over my leg. He presses his cheek against mine. "Vivie, babe, I need you to try not to project so much. I can't think."

I lift a hand to his silky hair, needing that connection. "Oh, God, no wonder you look like you're in pain. I'm sorry."

That's why he was screaming my name before he even arrived. He must have felt my pain from far away.

Breckin smiles. "Don't be crazy. I'd project, too."

Sitting back, he grabs my leg and closes his eyes. I focus my breathing, reeling back all my thoughts to keep him from feeling them. It only takes a moment for the light to emanate from his hands and my bones to mend. There's a muted click, like two building blocks being snapped back in place, then the heat is gone and the pain is no longer, and I burst into tears.

"Viv?" Breckin grabs my shoulders and draws me into his chest as he perches on the edge of the bed.

My nails scratch at his bare back as I try to hold him tighter. Zeke's face, the wicked smile he wore right before Hamon appeared—his plans for me were not noble. Another moment and who knows what would have happened? I lift my head, wiping my running nose and the deluge of tears on my sleeve as I look for Hamon.

He's retreated closer to the bedroom door, his arms crossed over his chest. His face may be neutral, but his eyes take in everything. I want to hate him for the father he is to Breckin, and yet he saved me.

"Thank you," I tell him, though the words don't come out. He must read my lips because he nods.

"Breckin, Hamon?" Elias yells, the front door slamming shut behind him.

Breckin looks toward the door, and Hamon waves him off. "Take a minute."

The moment the door closes behind Hamon, my face is in Breckin's hands. "Who is Zeke?"

"I don't know," I manage between shaky breaths. "He was in the square, just watching us. I felt him, and then he appeared before me and grabbed me." I relay everything that happened up until the moment he arrived on the porch. "Oh gosh, Zara. She was with me—"

Breckin holds me down when I try sitting up. "I'm sure she's fine. He probably just sent her off. We'll find her and make sure."

"I dropped my phone."

A half smile appears. "If that's all you lost, I'm happy to buy you another." His thumb brushes my cheek. "Your pain rushed in so suddenly. I had no idea what happened. I just knew something was wrong. I don't . . . Hamon just appeared?"

"He did."

There's a knock at the door.

"Breckin?" Elias pops his head in.

"Yeah, come in. She's fine." Dropping a kiss on the top of my head, Breckin peels himself from my arms. "You're a mess. Let me get a washcloth."

"How chivalrous of you to remark on my looks after what I just went through," I say with a frown. Breckin grimaces, and I fall into the pillows behind my back. My gaze strays over Elias's shoulder. "Where's Hamon?" I ask.

Elias looks at Breckin before he answers. "He didn't want to bring any more attention here than he might have already, so he left."

"Any more attention?"

"I told you we're in hiding here," Breckin says as the water turns off in the bathroom. "Hamon has kept my existence a secret for almost eighteen years. Or so he says."

"Breckin." Elias's warning tells me this isn't the first time they've had this discussion.

"I don't understand. He's barely visited Breckin in all his years here, but he happened to be close enough to swoop in and save me today?"

"He was hunting the hunter," Elias explains.

Goosebumps break out across my skin as Breckin returns to the side of my bed and hands me a cloth. I swipe at my face with the warm material as he uses another to wipe my knees. Every cut and scratch on my palms is gone, and my legs are perfect, too. His healing is effective, and I'm grateful.

"Is that what he said?" Breckin asks Elias after a moment. "Are we sure he isn't behind this attack? Maybe striking her was done to weaken me."

"Is that what you think of me, son?" Our heads swivel to the door to find Hamon standing there.

"Back so soon?" asks Breckin, snidely. Clearly his distrust for Hamon runs deep.

Hamon just smiles a smile so similar to his son's, I don't know how

Breckin doesn't recognize it. "I was halfway out of town when I realized it was time for you to stop hiding and me to stop running."

WALK ON WATER

BRECKIN

*a*s if the emotions from hearing Vivienne's terror weren't enough, my father now wants to show up and make amends? Vivienne's hand slips into mine, pumping twice.

Trying to maintain a calm façade, I ask, "Is your being here a danger to Viv?"

Hamon's gaze flicks between us. "It is. It's a danger to both of you."

I step forward. "Then leave."

"Breckin." Elias lifts his hands.

"Don't. My first priority is her, Elias. You know this." I suck in a deep breath and look at my father. I hate calling him that. "I will not go with you in April. I will not choose to join your fallen. I'm not aligning with them."

Hamon huffs. "Did you make this decision because of her? Your soul mate?"

"No, I made the decision a long time ago, but she is my main concern now. I'm not you, Hamon. I want redemption."

"My son, you do not know me well enough to say whether you are like me or not. In fact, I would say you are much more like me than you realize."

Elias remains still. His body tenses as his gaze volleys between

72

Hamon and me. Behind me, Vivienne squirms on the bed, but her hand doesn't leave mine.

"What if you had lost her today?" he asks. His amber eyes hold me hostage, and my hand tightens around Vivienne's as a precaution. "What if she was ended and you were forced to continue on, knowing you were not there to save her?"

"I would bring armies of terror down on those who took her from me," I say unequivocally.

He tips his head and turns. "Then we understand one another," he says as he leaves the room.

I pull my hand from Vivienne's and hurry after him. His long legs carry him through the house and out the back door with haste. I hesitate to speak. My mind is at war with the pros and cons of him being here. He hasn't offered me answers for seventeen years. Why would today change anything? Then the vision of Vivienne in his arms assaults me, and I need to know. "Why?"

His wings snap taut, and his muscles flex, ready for takeoff. At the last moment, as his knees give and he jumps into the air, he turns his head. His amber eyes meet mine, the hint of red glowing like wildfire. "Because you love her."

"Nothing I did worked." Vivienne's talking to Elias in the bedroom as I reenter the house. "Maybe it was my fear that kept me from reaching inside."

"Or maybe we were wrong. You might not have access to your angel the way Breckin does, or the way a full-blooded angel does," Elias counters.

"He transported. You told me angels had different gifts, but I didn't—" Her voice drops, then picks up again in low murmurs. I don't push my senses to catch her words. I give her her private fears, knowing she'll tell me if she wants me to hear them. Instead of returning to her side, I take a seat on the couch. There are fallen lurking around town, Vivienne was attacked, and Hamon saved her. *Because you love her.* Did he truly save her for me?

~

VIVIENNE REFUSES to do anything that could harm an innocent after her brush with Zeke. She cuts off Zara and everyone else. To help smooth things over, I use compulsion, keeping her friends busy with other things when they approach her. The lying and seclusion takes a toll.

"Is this how you felt?" Vivienne asks as we're driving away from school one afternoon.

"Is what—" I stop my question when I catch the longing gaze she has focused on a group of students screwing around in the parking lot. It's drizzling and cold, but that doesn't stop their laughter and playfulness. "Did you want to go with them?"

The group is mainly seniors, piling into cars and heading to the Burger Bar for after-school shakes and fries. The closer we come to graduation, the more they seem to be doing that. Like the reality of the end is upon them. Vivienne shakes her head, and I press the brakes.

Throwing my arm over the back of her seat, I turn to her. "Viv, nothing will happen if you want to be with your friends. Elias explained the event with Zeke. It was a one-time deal."

Her head swings my way slowly. "You can't lie to me anymore, Breck." *Damn it.* Soul bond connections are annoying. "I can't protect myself, I can't protect others, and I can't protect you. I'd rather go home."

Weeks pass this way. As my senses and power strengthen rapidly, Vivienne makes no progress with hers—other than those connected to our bond.

At the end of March, two weeks before my birthday, I drop Vivienne at her apartment after school.

"Why's Elias here?" she asks, climbing out of my Bronco.

I school my features. "Because he's going to stand guard for a few hours while I set things up."

"Set things up?" Her brow arches. "What things?"

"You'll see. Just do your homework and get ready for a date. Elias is going to bring you to my place at seven, okay?"

VIVIENNE ARRIVES with Elias at seven on the dot and doesn't make it through the door from the garage into the house before Zara mows her over.

"Z?" Vivienne looks for me over her best friend's shoulder as they hug.

"Surprise! Your Romeo of a boyfriend here planned this whole thing. God, I feel like I haven't seen you in weeks."

Vivienne forces a smile as Zara draws her toward the living room. "I see you every day at school."

"Well, it doesn't feel like it. This house is amazing, Viv. Breckin gave me the grand tour. No wonder you two spend so much time here instead of hanging out with the rest of us. We should totally have a party." Zara looks back at me, and I shake my head. I catch her whisper, "Convince him."

I grill cheeseburgers, while Vivienne and Zara use the deep fryer I bought to make fries. We sit around the table and talk about people at school, college, television shows, and celebrities. Mostly the girls talk and I nod, or frown when they bring up how hot certain actors are.

I'm taking a bite of my burger when I bite into something sour. "Ew. Viv, did you put pickles on my burger?" I pull off the bun and tomato and find four offending pickle chips.

She stops with a fry mid-air. "Of course I did."

"Of course you did? Why do you say it like that? Are pickles a burger requirement?" I tease.

Zara and Vivienne give me identical *are you an alien from outer space* looks. "Your boyfriend doesn't like pickles, Viv?"

"I didn't know. We've never . . . gosh, yeah I guess I never noticed him not eat them." She reaches over the table and plucks the pickles from my food. "There."

"There?" I ask incredulously. "I can't eat it now. It's contaminated. I'll have to make another."

"You're kidding, right?" Vivienne asks, gaping.

I get up from the table. "Nope. I hate pickles. Hate."

"Breckin, you've never once offered me your pickle."

Zara giggles, and I close my eyes, counting to five before I dare answer her.

"What are you talking about?" I ask, a little worried about their answer.

Zara huffs, like she can't understand why they need to explain this to me. "It's common knowledge that the pickle-challenged should offer the pickle-lover their pickle whenever they have one," she says with superiority.

For crying out loud. I rub the back of my neck.

"Whenever we go to the deli or Burger Bar, you get a pickle on your plate, and you've never offered it to me. I can't believe I didn't notice."

"And I'd be a little scared of you if you had," I mutter as I make a new cheeseburger.

Something hits my shoulder, and I turn to find a fry on the floor at my feet. I mentally add pickles to the long list of things Vivienne is crazy about, along with sweets, Napoli's pizza, and all the coffee drinks that taste like pure sugar.

At the end of the night, Operation Cheer Vivienne Up is a success, and for the first time in weeks, she falls asleep with a slight smile.

MY DEMONS

BRECKIN

"*B*reckin?"

I'm lying on Vivienne's bed the next night while she showers when Rachel walks into the bedroom. Thankfully, I was already cloaked. She invited me over for a movie and dinner, her famous grilled cheese sandwiches, with pickles on the side, and tomato soup, but as far as she knows, I left the apartment twenty minutes ago. Which I did, but I'm back as usual, still refusing to leave Vivienne unprotected at night.

I draw my wings closer to my spine as her mother stands in the doorway. Her eyes scan the seemingly empty room.

"I know you're here. You come back every night. You can show yourself."

My heart leaps to my throat. *Shit. Is she playing me?* I shift into a sitting position and wait for her to check under the bed or open the closet, but she doesn't. She steals a glance at Vivienne's closed bathroom door, then cracks a parent's smile.

"I'm not exactly sure how it works, but I know you can hide yourself from sight. I'd like to assume that's what you're doing right now and that you're not in the bathroom with my daughter, because that would cause issues between us." She walks farther into the room. My stomach hits the floor, and my wings bristle. What exactly does she know? "I've kept quiet because I knew you were protecting her, but I think we should talk, angel."

I drop the cloak, and she jumps as I appear. Her palm slaps at her chest, her audible gasp telling me she's startled, though the glint in her eyes says she's not surprised. It doesn't matter. I can erase this entire scene from her mind whenever I want. If she's holding something back—if she knows something—I want to know what it is.

"You knew?" I ask.

"That our town is full of things we don't speak of, or that you're a Nephilim?" Her gaze lingers on my dark wings. I don't respond, so she continues. "I have a journal, handed down from generation to generation. I know my family's heritage. And I know my daughter is different since meeting you."

Whoa. That's a revelation. "You have a journal? Viv's never seen it?"

"Of course not. If she were like the rest of us, she wouldn't have the need to know, at least not until she was older. What happened, Breckin?"

"I don't know what you're asking me."

"Yes, you do." She sits beside me on Vivienne's bed. "I was a headstrong teen. I'd lost my mother, and I never had a father. I was lost, then I came upon the journal in my mother's things as I was packing them away. Six generations of women starting with Phaedra. The angel." Rachel rubbed her hands together nervously. "None of them displayed the angelic attributes. Phaedra kept the journal on herself, her daughter, and her granddaughter, Lola. Then Lola took over, and it must have been passed down after that. Each woman kept notes. They all lived in this crazy town and knew of different aspects of it, but they kept it to themselves, preferring to live like an unknowing human.

"When I found the journal, I became obsessed with what it meant. I grew up friends with Rose Howe—"

The Howes are witches. Rose's daughter, Scarlet, is a junior at Havenwood Falls High and belongs to one of the only integrated social groups at the school, electing to hang out with both wolf and dragon shifters, and a fae. It caused a scandal at the beginning of the school year among some of the supes.

"Rose and I would sneak through her mother's books looking for anything we could find about awakening my angel DNA, but I imagine magic like that was locked away. So I tried other ways to figure out how to tap into what I am. Nothing worked, and eventually I left this town. I should make it clear to you that everything I'd learned about the supernatural here—my friendship with Rose, anything about this town, our heritage—it all disappeared from the journal, and from my memories, once I left Havenwood Falls. It wasn't until I returned that the journal was restored and my memories returned. There I was in Denver, with no background and nothing but vague memories of my life. So, I went to school and moved on."

I waited for the *until* in her words, but the water turned off in the bathroom. Rachel frowned.

"Breckin, since you started coming around, things have been different. When Viv and I are together, I feel a tug in my chest. I love my daughter, but it's not that sort of tug. It's a feeling like something is trapped in there, trying to claw its way out."

I run my hand through my hair, thinking. With the knowledge that we can erase her memories if this backfires, I close my eyes and project my thoughts toward Vivienne. *Your mother knows about me, and you.* Something heavy hits the floor followed by Vivienne's muttered curse. Confident she heard me, I fill Rachel in.

"On December eighth, I spotted Viv injured on her normal running trail up on Mount Alexa. She was bleeding heavily from an animal attack, and I didn't think she was going to make it."

Rachel's eyes tear up.

"I healed her, and as far as we can tell, that healing woke the angel within." Vivienne opens the bathroom door. She's chewing on her bottom lip as she looks at us sitting on her bed. Me with my wings in plain view. "It wasn't just her angelic blood that awoke that day, Rachel. There's something more between Viv and me, something stronger. We're soul mates."

"Why didn't you tell me?" Rachel stands and moves toward the bathroom doorway, pulling Vivienne from her rooted spot and hugging her. "I thought we shared everything."

"Everything?" Vivienne leaned back. "In my mind, telling my mother, whom I assumed was as normal as I once was, that I was evolving into an angel and I had a half-angel soul mate, sounded like something that would land me a trip to the looney bin."

Rachel's forehead creased as she shook her head. "Viv, you nearly died and you kept it from me?"

"And you apparently knew my boyfriend is an angel and you elected not to tell me."

"Wait—" I speak over their bickering, standing as a question knocks at the back of my mind, looking for an answer. "How *did* you know about me?"

How does one journal, a young witch, and some strange feelings add up to uncovering my secret? How did she make that leap?

Vivienne steps from her mother's embrace and comes to my side as Rachel smiles.

"Elias is your guardian and your father is Hamon," she says, like it's obvious. "Phaedra wrote about them both."

My palms prickle with excitement. She wrote about them? I could get the story from someone who would have no reason to lie to me, no reason to sugarcoat things. "Can I see it? Can I see the journal?"

Vivienne's hand touches my lower back.

Rachel shrugs one shoulder. "Sure, I don't see why not. There is one other thing, though. Another reason I was suspicious." Her fingers go to her collar, playing with the fabric as she looks at Vivienne. Nervousness exudes from her pores. "There was one other time when I felt that strange tugging I described to you."

Her words hang in the air.

"I felt it when I was with Vivienne's father."

ELASTIC HEART

VIVIENNE

When Breckin sent me the message saying Mom knows we're angels, I knocked a shampoo bottle onto my toe. He had to be teasing. Toweling off from my shower, I throw on the clothes I wear to sleep and open the door to find them sitting on my bed. Breckin's wings are on full display, and Mom is not on the floor in shock. When did this become my life?

Why didn't you tell me?

Um, hello? Why in the hell did you not tell me about the journal, about the angel genes, about our family's connection with Hamon and Elias, and finally . . . *the odd feelings you had with the man who gifted you me!*

Breckin chuckles, and my gaze snaps to his face. His mouth is taut. He's laughing in his head—at me and my flurry of thoughts. I pinch his nonexistent love handle.

Where do I begin with her?

"What do you mean you felt the same sensation Viv gives you with her father?" Breckin asks, and bless him for saying something because my mouth feels as though it's filled with sawdust.

Mom clasps her hands over her head and pushes her hair back with a deep sigh. Her blue eyes plead with mine when she faces me. "I'm sorry I didn't tell you."

"Tell me what?" I ask, punctuating each word.

"I didn't go after him. He found me in a bar. Nothing special, but when I saw what he was, I didn't walk away. I'd hoped—"

Anticipation sends a wave of electricity across my skin. I'm antsy and itchy and altogether uncomfortable about what she might say.

"He was an angel, Viv."

"That's impossible." I turn to Breckin. "Isn't that impossible?"

"I . . . uh, I don't know. I've been told not all Nephilim have angelic traits, but considering . . ." He trails off.

For weeks now, Elias has told me that the easiest way to tap into my angel side was when my emotions are high. If there's ever the perfect time, this is it. The porcelain angel from my childhood returns to my memory. No wonder she got rid of it one year without warning. It must have freaked her out watching me stare at it so obsessively.

"Viv, sweetie?" Hands touch my arms, and I slap them away.

"Don't," my voice says, but I'm not here. I'm floating above this scene. My emotions are too frantic to process. My father was an angel. My mother knew. She lied to me.

"Vivie?" I turn my face into the heat that is Breckin's touch on my cheek. His snow-and-pine scent comforts me. "Clear your thoughts. This is just another hurdle we'll figure out together." I blink twice, and his face comes into focus. "Hey, you," he says with a smile.

My bottom lip trembles at the tenderness.

"We've got this, Viv." His brows lift like he's verifying I'm all right.

"Yeah. Yeah, I'm okay."

He leans closer and brushes a kiss near my temple. "I'm going to call Elias."

I'm cold the minute Breckin leaves the room. I walk around my bed and look out my window. A light snow falls, the white flakes sparkling as they hit the ground. I'm so ready for spring.

"What was his name?" I ask, keeping my gaze outside. "Was it Sam, or was that a lie too?"

Her reflection in the glass moves closer. "That was the name he gave me."

"And he showed himself to you? That's how you know he was an angel?"

She moves closer. "Viv, sit with me," she says softly as her hand closes around mine.

We move to my bed, and I climb into the middle and sit cross-legged while she pulls one leg up and hangs the other off the side. There are dark shadows under her eyes. She slept today, but working nights takes its toll on her. Or maybe the tired look has more to do with me lately.

"You're not a child anymore, but I still hate admitting my failures to you. I was alone in Denver. Sure, I'd made friends, but I was unhappy. I had no family. Your father cozied up to me one night at a bar when I needed someone to talk to. He was charming, and gorgeous, and I felt drawn to him. I did try to walk away, but he followed after me.

"That was when I saw what he was. We'd been dancing, and that tug I told Breckin about, it wouldn't stop. I remember the ache still. I thought I was having a heart attack at twenty-two."

I bite the inside of my cheek and rub my palm over my own heart. "I know it well," I tell her. "When I'm away from Breckin, I can't get back to him quick enough. The angel side of me fights to be with him. I have no power over it."

Her eyes shine. "You're not supposed to be that in love at seventeen," she says with a hint of sadness. "You're your own person now. You don't need me anymore."

"That isn't true. I'll always need a mom." My free hand covers our clasped ones. "I just need a mom who will be truthful with me."

With a sniff, she continues, "That feeling scared me, Viv. I ran from him and hurried to my car. I was about to start my engine when he appeared in the parking lot. He was searching for me, his head turning every which way, and that's when I saw his wings. He turned, and they shot out of his back, these massive black wings with midnight blue and deep purples streaking the shiny feathers. I got maybe fifteen seconds before he disappeared"—she snaps her fingers—"poof. Like that.

"For some reason, I didn't freak out and hightail it out of there. Something deep inside me knew that him being an angel wasn't so out of the ordinary. I went back inside. I went back to the bar, sat down, and waited. Soon enough, he showed up. After a few drinks, I took him home with me."

When a child asks how their parents met, they expect to hear some funny tidbit followed by a love story, or something about sparks igniting and eyes never straying again . . . they don't expect to hear the sordid details of a one night stand.

"No wonder you gave me so many safe-sex talks growing up."

"He didn't use his powers against me, Viv. He may have used his charm to get me to dance and to get a few kisses, but once I saw his wings, I wanted that moment with him. I'm ashamed to admit it excited me."

"Well, I would say you got excitement, about nine months later, right?" I say, not kindly.

"Viv?" Breckin knocks on the frame of my bedroom door. "Sorry, I talked to Elias, and we're thinking you two should come over to the house for the night."

"Yeah, we can do that," I reply, not giving Mom the chance to argue. She rubs her palms down her thighs and stands with me, giving me a nod of consent.

THIRTY MINUTES LATER, we're parking Mom's car in Breckin's garage next to his Bronco. Mom and I have lived in our little two-bedroom apartment forever, and seeing the open awe on her face as Breckin walks us through his beautiful home hurts my heart. She loves beauty as much as I do, but money is scarce.

We stop at the staircase to the basement. Breckin touches my back. "Want to take her downstairs? I'll be right there."

"So this is where you two spend all your time?" she asks as I flip the light switch and lead her into what has become my safe space.

"There's a bathroom and bedroom over there, a full kitchen." I point everything out for her. "I'll put our bags in the guest room, since I'm sure that's where he wants us."

"Is his house warded or protected somehow? Is that why he wanted you here?"

"Us, Mom," I call over my shoulder as I drop our bags on the large bed. "He wants us here. And I don't know if it's protected. He's always brought me down here. I think having only one way in or out, and it being underground helps him feel like he can better protect me."

"And can he? Protect you?"

"I will, or I'll die trying," answers Breckin as he descends the staircase with Elias at his back.

Mom stiffens. "Can you die? I mean differently than a full-blooded angel?"

The idea is a knife through my chest.

"He won't die," I say. My head held high, I look at Breckin like I'm ordering him to survive whatever comes our way. Death is not an option. I want forever with this angel. He winks, and a thrilling surge of tingles run up my spine.

Feeling slightly mollified, now that I've made my position clear on his leaving me, I introduce Elias. It's a silly formality, because they've known each other around town for years, and he's watched her and our family line since before either of us were born, as Breckin explained to her on our drive here. She said she already knew, because of Phaedra's journal.

"So I understand you are the reason I've made it through life relatively unscathed?" Mom asks, her voice shaking. "I have to admit, once I knew I had my own guardian angel, I was a little more careless with myself."

The gruff angel flashes a half smile filled with emotion before he motions toward the couch. "Shall we?"

Breckin and I exchange looks. What did he and Elias speak about before they came downstairs? Breckin sits in the oversized chair closest to the fireplace, grabbing my hand and pulling me into the space next to him, as Mom takes the couch and Elias takes the other chair closer to her.

"We should let them speak," Breckin whispers as his arm goes around my shoulders and tucks me into his side.

Their body language is uncomfortable times one thousand as they settle into their seats. Mom presses a hand to her throat, her forehead wrinkling as she studies Elias.

"I would like to read Phaedra's journal," Elias finally says, scratching the beard at his jaw.

"Of course."

As if that agreement from my mother was all he needed, Elias relaxes. His shoulders fall, and he sinks back into his chair.

"Rachel, we need to know about Viv's father. I'm sure it's not easy to talk about, but if he was an angel . . ." He trails off, a wave of emotions once again sweeping over his features.

Rubbing her arms and tucking her legs up beside her, she begins. "We met at this bar in Denver . . ."

Elias listens intently to the almost word-for-word retelling of the story she gave me in my bedroom at the apartment. Breckin's attention to her story tells me he didn't listen in on us after he left my room to make his phone call. His fingers play mindlessly up and down my bicep as he listens, making my eyes heavy. Like Elias, he remains silent, but his expressive face gives me all the clues I need to know what's playing in his mind. There are too many unanswered questions for his liking.

"And you never saw him again?" Elias asks when she finishes.

"I did not."

"Viv's birth was hard on you," Elias states rather than asks.

That nudges me from the sleepy spell Breckin's caress put me in. "It was?"

Of course Elias knows. He watched over us.

Mom's wide gaze shifts to Breckin and me like she forgot we're here. "It wasn't easy, but you were worth it."

Her soft smile says so much. The pain, the uncertainty . . . the love she feels for me is worth it all. My arm tightens around Breckin's stomach. I know the feeling well.

"It makes sense. I'm unaware of a human living after giving birth to an angel's child, but you did. That part of you that holds Phaedra's blood must have protected you."

"Wait," Breckin says. "What does that mean for Viv? Will having kids be difficult for her?"

Mom chokes as Elias releases a throaty growl. "Is that a concern right now?" he asks with a scowl.

I'm shaking my head and sitting up, but Breckin has apparently lost his mind. "Well, at this moment, no, but since we're discussing it . . . it's something I'd like to know. I wouldn't want to put her at risk."

I hiss his name as the mom glare hits me from across the room.

"You do know the sure way to keep her from risk, don't you, Breckin?" Elias asks tersely.

"I'm not sure if I remember. Will you remind me?"

Mom gives a dainty snort, breaking the tension in the room, and I shove Breckin sideways. Elias shakes his head with a light laugh.

"We don't need to discuss any of this right now. No concerns. None at all," I reiterate, giving Mom a serious look. "I'm barely adjusting to the idea of not being human, let alone the idea of having little angel babies someday."

Breckin's jaw drops. "You don't want to have little Breckins with me?"

"Breckin," Elias snaps. "Can we please be serious here?"

"I am being serious. I have every intention of marrying this girl and having a big, happy, normal angel family someday."

My eyes roll because he's being ridiculous, but it's also ridiculously sweet, and I do want that. I want a future with him.

We'll have one, he says in my head.

Elias and Mom share an unreadable look. Parent looks, I suppose. This wasn't the future Mom and I dreamed about over the years, but it's the one presenting itself. If we make it through the next few weeks.

"So, what about the feeling Rachel described?" Breckin asks, getting back to the real point of our meeting. "It sounds similar to the tug between Viv and me. Could it—"

"We don't have souls, Breckin. You know that." Elias steeples his fingers. "Maybe it was some other bond, though? I'm not sure."

Mom clears her throat. "I feel it now." She meets Elias's blue eyes and tilts her head, her hand once again going to her throat. "I've felt it since the moment you walked in."

ON MY OWN

BRECKIN

*E*lias jerks backward like he's been slapped. His jaw drops.

"It's not romantic in nature," Rachel rushes. "It's just . . . gravitational. It's strongest when I'm around Viv, but I've felt it around Breckin, too."

"What?" I sit forward, nearly knocking Vivienne to the floor in my haste. I shoot her an apologetic grin and turn back to her mother. "Why? What? Why?"

Vivienne squeezes my thigh. "You said those words already."

Elias blows out a deep breath and stands to pace the room.

"In all the years I've been around you on and off, Elias, I've never felt it. Same with Breckin"—she looks at me—"I didn't notice anything until the last few weeks. I thought maybe it was because you were around more often. I know you're an angel, so I didn't think much about it."

"Viv's angel side is trying to talk to yours," Elias says. He stops pacing, his gaze meeting each of ours. "You share the same makeup. She knows it's in there, and she's talking to you."

Well, shit. "That's horror movie kind of stuff," I say with a cringe.

"No, Breckin, that's celestial kind of stuff. Angels were created as brothers and sisters. We call for each other naturally." His mouth twists, then he looks to Rachel again. "Maybe you're feeling this tug to Breckin and me because of Phaedra. We were . . . close."

Her name drips with pain every time it leaves his lips. What exactly is their story? And how does Hamon fit into it?

"Okay, but wait." Vivienne holds up a hand. "I hear what you're saying, Elias. Mom and I share the same blood, so my angelic side talks to hers. I guess I can see where maybe it's waking hers up, like Breckin woke mine. And hers is trying to get to you two because you're you, and well, Breckin has Hamon's blood. You were all connected." She ticks off each point on her fingers, her forehead creased. "But what about my father? Why would she have felt that way with him? Especially way back then, when her gene was still asleep. Where's the connection?"

Elias nods thoughtfully, taking in her points. "I'm not sure we're going to have all the answers. Everything is speculation here. It always has been."

Could there not be some Angel 101 book lying around that would tell us how this all works? They were created, they fell, they're cut off. Those are the only absolutes I've ever known. Hell, even us thinking we're soul mates may not be accurate. Maybe the bond we share is something else. Maybe it wasn't my healing Vivienne that changed her —maybe Death did. There is no one who can tell us for sure what we want to know. Elias goes by what he's seen through centuries of living, much of which he's never adequately described to me, because he says there is no way to adequately describe the creation of the world and his place in it before he came here.

Rachel rubs her arms as she stands. "Let me get the journal for you."

Elias's gaze tracks her movement across the room, his face blank. Once she disappears into the guest bedroom, he turns to the fireplace and stares into the flames with a deep frown.

I move to his side and watch the fire with him. "If her father is an angel, why didn't she show any signs? Hell, she's got the blood of two angels within . . . shouldn't she have developed some gifts?"

He massages the back of his neck. "I understand Phaedra, but—"

"Why?" I hiss a little harsher than intended. From the corner of my eye, I catch Vivienne stand. Her brows reach her hairline, lifted in question, as she joins us. She hates being left out of these things. Lacing my pinky and ring finger with hers, I ask Elias the question I probably should have asked weeks ago. "There isn't an age to our angelic blood. You've told me that before. It doesn't pass down the way traits do in humans. It doesn't get weaker the further you are from the original DNA, right?" The wrinkles at the edge of Elias's eyes deepen, and I forge on. "So my child, and his, and his, and his, forever and ever will always bear Hamon's blood. Why was Phaedra's any different?"

Vivienne shakes her fingers free of mine and moves in front of Elias, putting her back to the fireplace. He's a good half a foot shorter than me, but he's still a head taller than her. Add in his bulky build next to her diminutive frame, and he looks like he could swallow her whole. Her delicate hand touches his arm tenderly. "Elias, I can tell the history you've kept from Breckin is painful. I'm sure you had a good reason for it, but now we need to know. You know we do."

He remains silent.

"You said she was stripped of her angelic markers. What does that mean? How does that even happen?" Vivienne asks.

His look is all the answer I need, but Vivienne can't read him the way I can.

"It was God, Vivie," I say as Rachel returns to the room. "The Creator punished her. There is no other way to strip an angel of their power. They're divine. Even the fallen and damned don't lose all their abilities. They just use them for the wrong purposes."

"What did she do that was so bad?" Vivienne's face mirrored Elias's. Pain. The kind of pain that embeds into the marrow of your bones and siphons you dry. He turns away, his head dropping.

"She never would tell me," he confesses, the rasp of his voice scratching across my heart. *Why so much pain?* Even Vivienne swipes at the lashes beneath her eyes as she looks from me to her mother.

"Actually," Rachel says, speaking with the subdued tone of a medical professional who has relayed diagnoses—both bad and good

—hundreds of times to overwrought families. She holds out an accordion style binder. "I keep everything in here. The original entries are tattered and difficult to read, but along the way, they were rewritten. I suppose to preserve the words. She wrote it all in there."

Elias barely glances up as he takes the binder into his hands. "Thank you."

For the longest time the only sound in the room comes from the soft flames of the gas fire. I break the silence. "Go."

Realizing he has been the focus of three pairs of eyes, Elias straightens.

"Go on upstairs and read it. We can talk more tomorrow."

With a murmured goodnight, Elias leaves, taking the steps two at a time and closing the door at the top. Vivienne leans against my back and yawns. It's three in the morning.

Reaching behind my back and pulling her arm around my waist, I rub her forearm.

"You two should probably get some sleep," I suggest. Rachel laughs softly. Clearly, a seventeen-year-old telling her to go to bed is humorous. "Sorry, I don't mean to be disrespectful."

Rachel's already waving my apology off when Vivienne butts in. "Sure he does. Breckin has a thing with being overprotective. You'll get used to it, Mom." She stretches to her toes and kisses my cheek. "I'm gonna brush my teeth, then you can wash up," she tells her mother.

"Thank you for that, Breckin." Rachel's voice pulls my gaze from watching Vivienne's backside walk away.

"I feel like I'm the one who should be thanking you"—I smile and jerk my head toward the bathroom—"for that."

She gives a huff of laughter. "You love her."

"More than anything." I can't express that sentiment strongly enough. "It sounds stupid, doesn't it? We're teens."

"Well, you're not exactly normal teens, though, are you?"

"No, we aren't. I grew up knowing about Heaven and Hell. The real stories. And Viv . . . well, she's pretty focused."

"Breckin, you don't have to justify yourselves. I can see how much you care for each other. I appreciate the way you protect my daughter, especially now. It was my biggest fear when I became pregnant. It's why I remained in Havenwood Falls after I came back. I wanted to protect her from him."

Which reminds me. "How did you make your way back here? You said your memories were gone." As angels, or half angels, the wards don't work on us, but Phaedra's gene wasn't active in Rachel before Vivienne's came alive. No one recognized the Freemans for the angel gene they had within.

Rachel nods. "The wards . . . yes. I have two theories on that. My best answer is your uncle, as Viv likes to call him. Elias watched over me back then, right? Perhaps he compelled me to return when he saw my predicament?"

That makes sense. Elias would have wanted Rachel here, where he felt it safest for her.

"And second," she says, ticking off each thought on her fingers, "in the journal, Phaedra wrote about a promise she made to three witches to protect and watch over a canyon. A canyon that became the seat of Havenwood Falls much later."

Seems like Rachel has had the answers to Vivienne's quest for the history of her family and this town all along. "So you think maybe her promise to them forged a bond between your family line and the magic here?"

"Perhaps." She rubs her arms. "Breckin, there are things in that journal . . . explanations Phaedra made that will affect Elias and Hamon. For the better, I think. I—"

The lock on the bathroom door snaps, and Vivienne walks out. "Your turn."

Rachel looks at me and smiles. Whatever she intended to say fades as she pats Vivienne's head and grabs her things before heading into the bathroom.

When the bathroom door clicks closed, Vivienne grins. She pulls on the sleeves of her nightshirt, tugging them over her palms. The mischievous gleam in her eyes awakens the angel, who's behaved so well tonight. The taste of her minty mouth is permanently etched on my tongue. I long to draw her close and dive in.

"So, where are you going to be while I'm in there?" she asks, pointing toward the guest room.

I've been by her side every night since the week I healed her. That's over one hundred days of feeling her heart beat while she sleeps.

"I guess I'll be setting up camp on the couch here."

"This couch?" she purrs, her hand skimming along my side and around my back as she circles me and moves around to the front of the couch. "This very wide couch that I already know from personal experience can fit two people comfortably?"

"Vivie?"

With a wink, she scurries into the other room, returning with pillows and a blanket. Tossing the pillows on the couch, she tugs at me. When I resist, she pouts prettily. "I want to be with you."

The angel takes the bait. Snatching her close, my fingers press into her hips. "Me, too, but your mom—"

"Will be fine. We're just laying here. Sleep, nothing more."

She has no idea how difficult that is. While she sleeps, her soft body pressed up against mine, I lay awake imagining all the things that I want to do to her.

"Breckin," she gasps, her eyes wide. "Do you really?"

"Do I really what?" I ask, confused, then it hits me. "Crap, you heard my thoughts, didn't you?" The apples of her porcelain cheeks stain pink as she nods. "I'm sorry—"

My apology dies as a vision of the two of us together pops into my mind. My spine vibrates with the need to release my wings as Vivienne's skin shines in the moonlight. We're on a beach, the waves lapping at our skin as our mouths, then bodies, come together in pure bliss.

"That's what I see"—she cups my cheek and the vision dies—"someday, Breck. Just us. We don't have to rush this, because I know it will happen, and it will be divine perfection."

Divine perfection. That is what we are. Souls destined to meet, angels destined to love. We come from the fallen and the damned, and yet we've been given *this.*

I brush her lips carefully. "Someday."

THE DARK OF YOU

VIVIENNE

"*D*o you feel a vibration within your chest? Like a pulse, humming with energy?"

I clench my eyes tighter and dig deeper. Imagining invisible fingers, I peel away skin and muscles in search of the missing piece. It's a game of Operation, my mind visualizing the tweezers picking through my body. She's there, somewhere within my makeup, but I can't reach her.

My head falls back to the couch, a deep exhale leaving my lungs. "I can't."

Breckin's hand rubs my knee. "How do you read my thoughts, or project your feelings to me?"

I rub my temples. "I don't know. That just happens. I don't control it."

"Vivie, we need to get to her. I need for you to be able to protect yourself. We have two weeks." Frustration coats his words.

"Do you think I don't know that?" I snap. Breckin leans forward with a low growl. He digs his fingers through his hair angrily, and I grab at his arm. "Sorry. I know you're trying to help. Why are you so grouchy about it this morning, though?"

. . .

I WOKE on the couch alone, the basement nearly black without windows to allow the morning sun. My mind struggled to place where I was, until I turned and saw Breckin's faint silhouette hovering over me. The fireplace burned on low behind him, and my heart slammed into my ribs at the haunted look he wore.

"Breckin?" I pushed to a sitting position and turned around. The guest bedroom door was closed. "What are you doing?"

"I need you to work on your abilities." His tone was serious.

"Okay. I have been working on them, but if—" He shakes his head before I finish, so I clamp my jaw shut.

"No, Vivienne. We need to work harder. I need you to access your power, if you have any."

"If?"

"Why aren't you feeling them? You are the blood of two angels. Obviously, it's in there—we've seen glimpses of it. You have to pull it out and take control."

"Damn it." He scrubs his hands over his face. We've been at this for more than an hour. He's attempted explaining the feelings until he's blue in the face, and I've concentrated so hard, my head wants to explode. Still nothing. "I had a . . . I guess it was a vision, last night."

His fingers bear down on his forehead like he can rub whatever image he sees out of his mind, and I purse my lips to stop from interrupting. My leg bounces as my nerves crank into gear.

"You were screaming. That's not even the right word. It was piercing. Your terror ripped me open and wrenched my heart out. There was so much . . ." His jaw clenched. "I just need you to be able to protect yourself. What if I can't be with you all the time? What if another Zeke shows up?"

"Who's Zeke?"

I spin at Mom's voice.

"No one." There's no reason to upset her. Breckin is upset enough for twenty overprotective mothers.

"He was a fallen who attacked Viv last month," Breckin says.

I throw him a dirty look as Mom walks around the couch and sinks to the edge of the chair, brows raised.

"Hamon killed him, but not before Zeke broke her leg in two places. I healed her," he further explains.

Anger mixed with fear burns in her eyes. "I thought you were protecting her."

"Mom." I wrap a hand around Breckin's thigh. "I forced him and Elias to let me go that day. They've followed me every second of every day since this whole thing began. I needed a day. I thought it would be fine."

Breckin ignores me and meets her gaze. "You're right, Rachel. I shouldn't have let her out of my sight. I won't make that mistake again, but even with me at her side . . . If we're attacked, she needs her own strength."

The urge to throw something hits me. I know I need my own strength, but maybe I don't have any. Maybe the glowing, and the speed, and the sensing other creatures were all flukes. Maybe I'm a lemon. The angel who would never be.

"Is there something after her? After either of you?" Mom asks.

Breckin's mouth opens, then closes as his head tips up. A moment later, the door opens from upstairs, and Elias comes down into the basement. His hair is a tangled mess, like he spent the night ripping his fingers through it. He snaps his attention to Mom, stopping in front of her, pages gripped in his hand.

"You took her to the Court?" Anger and accusation color his words. Breckin leaps to his feet and grabs at Elias's arm, but the older angel shrugs him off. "What did they do to her, Rachel? What did you have them do?"

"Elias." My voice isn't half as scary as his when I jump in front of him. Mom shrinks back in her chair, her face pale and eyes wide. "You have no right to speak to her that way."

The man who has always shown such care and calm around me looks like he wants to snap a few necks. I worry I'm one of them as his blue eyes scan my face. Our stares clash for what feels like a full minute before he shakes his head and slides back.

"Tell your daughter what you did."

Mom touches the back of my leg, nudging me to the side so she can stand. With her fists clenched at her sides, she holds her head high as she says, "I did what I thought I had to do to protect her."

The world spins.

"When I found out I'd become pregnant, the reality of what I'd done hit me. I had no idea what type of angel Sam was. I had no idea what she would be. I ran home, to Havenwood Falls, and I went to Rose for help."

Okay. I breathe in, then out. *Rose Howe, the witch. That's fine. She mentioned her friendship last night. Breathe, Viv.*

"And Rose brought me to the Court. I don't know who they were. They didn't let me see them, because I'm human. I don't know how Rose convinced them to speak with me, but she did. They felt the darkness."

"He's aligned with Hell?" Breckin asks as I stand there shocked.

Mom blinks. "Yes, they said he wasn't an angel of Heaven, but was damned. A demon of Hell."

I can't hold my temper. "Demon?" I gasp. "You said he was an angel. You saw his wings."

She's a deer in headlights as she looks between us. Clearly, she has no idea. She was a stupid young woman who slept with an angel in the hopes of awakening her own angelic gene. Apparently, she didn't have the sense to consider consequences, or protection, at the time.

Elias's hand falls on her shoulder, and I want to slap it off. *Don't comfort her. Look what she's done.* Tears blur my eyes.

"Viv," Elias says softly. "What the Court meant was fallen angels who align with Hell are no better than demons. They may be born of Heaven, but if they choose Hell, the darkness and corruption turns their insides to ash and flames. They're damned. They lose all chance of redemption."

My stomach cramps. *Does that make me . . . ? Am I . . .*

"The reaper," Breckin murmurs. With a curse, he stalks to the kitchen and slams his hand on the white marble countertop so hard, I'm afraid we'll find a crack later. "Sebastian knew she was different.

That night up on the mountain, he asked if she would join me or if she would turn her back on her calling. I assumed he was insulting me and saying he thought I was damned, because I'm Nephilim. That he was asking if I would turn her to Hell. But, that can't be . . . reapers can read our alliance. That's their job. Sebastian knew I had no plans of turning to Hell. He knew I wouldn't swear allegiance to Hamon."

Elias sucks in a breath. "The reaper used that knowledge to align himself with Hamon. That's why your father killed him."

Their explanations and line of thinking feel like a merry-go-round. I can't keep up. "You're saying Sebastian was actually asking if you would turn me away from Hell? He thought I was aligned with Hell, that Hell is my calling?"

Panic weighs me down. Elias and Mom speak at the same time, but my eyes lock on Breckin's, needing him to tell me what he thinks. His hands cup my face and draw me closer as he shakes his head. "Vivie, we can't trust anything he said, but the fact that he asked which way you would turn tells us he didn't know. I think that's why he wanted you so badly. Your allegiance isn't chosen."

My throat burns with unshed tears. "Sure it is." I cover his hands and press my forehead to his. "I choose you. I choose us."

"And I choose you. It doesn't matter who your father is."

"But is that why I'm not evolving?" I pull back and turn to Elias. "Would my father's blood stop Phaedra's?"

"No, it's all still celestial blood. You may have an affinity for darkness, thanks to his choice, but you're still part angel. The Court could have affected it, though," Elias says.

The Court. We're back where this began. Mom brought me to the Court, the true governing body of Havenwood Falls, as Breckin had explained before.

Elias waves the journal in his hand. "Rachel, you wrote in the journal that the Court said they would try to help her. What exactly did you ask of them?"

"I asked if they could help hide her. I knew about the memory wards on the town, and how they have spells to protect different species. I figured they had to have something that would keep her safe.

Keep anyone from knowing she is part angel. They took a sample of my blood, then they made me leave the room."

"I've never scented another angel gene in her . . . for the Court to hide it from us, they would need a lot of magic. They took your blood? They covered her parentage. It had to be a blood binding. I need to speak to them, find out who was there and what happened."

He's halfway up the stairs before Breckin runs after him. "E, wait!"

I shoot Mom a glance and take off after Breckin.

"What does that mean?" Breckin asks as I catch up to them by the front door.

Elias looks at me as he answers. "They probably bound your angel DNA up in your mother's blood. Covered it. Shifters and other creatures think you're human. We didn't notice, and I've been around you your entire life. It means that the reason you can't access your angel side could be because it's trapped within their spell. Breckin may have weakened the spell when he healed you, but your DNA is still tied up."

"Can that be reversed?" Breckin asks.

Elias waits for a beat before answering, "Most magic can, so I would think so, but there's a price."

"What price?"

"If your father is looking for you, Vivienne, or if the fallen or damned who know him find you—they will sense his blood in you. You won't be able to hide."

WAR OF HEARTS

BRECKIN

*I*t's been hours since Elias left. Vivienne and Rachel alternate between pleasant conversation and full on World War III battles, sending me from the basement to the first floor of the house. I wander the empty rooms, doing my best to keep my thoughts to myself.

Vivienne's father makes no difference to me. Fallen or damned, she is mine and she is good. My father, though . . . something Elias said downstairs nags at me.

"The reaper used that knowledge to align himself with Hamon. That's why your father killed him."

It meant little in the moment, with everything being thrown at us, but now . . . now I want to know more. Elias has pushed for me to talk to Hamon for weeks. I pull my cell phone from my pocket and pull up the number I have for him. My fingers hover over the keyboard. *What do I say?* I type out a text.

Thank you for saving Vivienne. We should talk.

It's not groundbreaking, but it's something. I've never reached out to him myself. Elias has been our connection my entire life. I didn't even have a way of reaching him until a year ago, when Elias was dealing with something for the Court and worried about me having no one if something should happen to him. At the time, I figured having no one wasn't much different than having Hamon. Maybe I shouldn't be so quick to judge anymore.

The binder Rachel handed Elias last night with Phaedra's story is nowhere to be found. I search drawers and closets, thinking he stuffed it away for safekeeping. The story has me curious. I could ask Rachel, but Elias's adamant refusal to tell me the entire story without Hamon present prevents me from doing so.

I rejoin Rachel and Vivienne downstairs, and we mindlessly watch television and wait in silence for Elias to return with news from the Court. Hamon never responds to my text.

It's after dark when the sound of Elias's truck pulling into the driveway has me charging upstairs. His face is ragged when he meets me at the back door.

"What's wrong?" My muscles flex at the stress rolling off him.

"Vivienne needs to come with me. The witches have agreed to undo the spell."

"So, there was a spell? What did they do?" I ask as Rachel and Vivienne's footsteps sound on the stairs. For a moment, I worry Elias won't speak. I'm so used to secrets between us, but this involves all of us.

Scattered thoughts invade my mind. *Vivienne.* She's flipping through every emotion possible with no filter. She doesn't have the control to keep them to herself. My wings strain against my skin, always yearning for her, as Elias blows out a deep breath.

"Yes, there was a spell. We can discuss it later. I need to take her now."

"Now?" Vivienne asks as she stands beside me. She wraps her arm around mine and leans into me. Rachel takes a spot on her other side, her face a mask of worry.

"Why the urgency, Elias?" I demand.

"I spoke to your father earlier, Breckin. There are things . . . We've been planning for issues to arise because of you, for years—"

I swallow the little moisture left in my dry mouth. "Issues because of me?"

"There's so much you don't know. The legions of damned would like more than anything to get the son of Hamon in their clutches. They know you exist now. There's been movement."

Zeke. Jack saying there were damned hanging around . . . "How?"

Elias's gaze lands on Vivienne, and she leans closer. "Sebastian didn't have to speak to many. He put the bug in someone's ear, and it moved through the chain. Hamon coming here to help you when he did, it brought attention to Havenwood Falls."

"I don't understand. Hamon is one of them. He works with the fallen. Why would they want Breckin? Why was it necessary to keep him in hiding all these years?" Vivienne asks.

"He works with the *fallen*, Viv. Not the damned," Elias points out. "There is a distinction. And we hid Breckin to protect him."

"From what?" Vivienne pushes.

Elias looks over his shoulder, and my gaze follows. Is he expecting something? I step forward, subtly shielding Vivienne. "Hamon's not who you think he is—"

"Stop." I draw away from Vivienne's grasp. "You keep saying that, but you never say more. I have seventeen years that say he's exactly what I think he is, E. If you want me to change my opinion, it's time you tell me what's going on."

Elias tosses his head back and sighs.

"Breckin," he says my name low. When he looks at me again, it's with all the understanding of the father he's been. He knows my struggles. He's been here for them. And he's been with Hamon since the beginning. Literally. He bridges the distance between us and clasps my arm affectionately. "He was trying to keep you safe, but by doing so, he forfeited his right to be what you needed him to be. He knows this. In the beginning, when you were born, I tried to get him to stay, but he was set on revenge."

"Revenge?" *Against whom?*

His hand squeezes my bicep. "Look, we don't have time to discuss this right now. I told Addie Viv and I would be at the meeting spot by now."

"Wait." Vivienne finally speaks up. "Addie? Addie Beaumont is a witch?"

Elias and I merely look at her, and she holds her hands up in surrender.

"We need to go," Elias says again.

"Fine. Let's grab shoes and coats and go. We can discuss Hamon on the way." I turn, but Elias stops me.

"Only Viv and I can go."

My gaze meets Vivienne's before I turn to Elias with a laugh. "I'm sorry?"

"You're not going."

"Like hell, I'm not going. You are not taking my soul mate to have some crazy ritual done by witches without me there."

Elias steps closer, his stocky physique making up for his lack of height when he stands in my face. His features harden. "You are not going."

Bad idea. The feeling screams at me. This isn't smart. I can't let her go. I step back, and Elias steps forward. He holds my gaze, his eyes silently telling me to calm down.

"I don't like this."

"I know you don't." He looks at Rachel and Vivienne, who are both standing there with different expressions. Vivienne watches me, her teeth tugging at her lip. Rachel's crossed her arms over her stomach, her mouth in a straight line. "The coven doesn't have to do this, Breckin. It's a favor. You know I won't let anything happen to her."

The vision I had while Vivienne slept replays. The darkness punctuated by her screams. "Give us a sec?" I ask.

Taking Vivienne's hand, I lead her to the office in the back of the house. It's the only room on the first floor that provides privacy, besides the guest room. Shutting the massive doors behind us, I lean against the wood and watch her.

"You think I should do this, right?" she asks after a moment.

"I don't know what other choice we have. If those witches did something to your blood that affects your angel side, we need it removed. I need you at one hundred percent." *All this time I've wondered why our soul bond didn't click sooner. Was it this spell?*

Her mouth twists. "What if this is me at one hundred percent?"

Before she can blink, I've grabbed her and twisted her around until she's pressed to the door and I'm hovering over her, my arms caging her in.

"Do you remember the first time we stood this way?" I ask, recalling the fear in her beautiful face that night.

She tugs my hips closer as she smiles. "You accosted me in the bathroom at Burger Bar."

"That I did." My lips brush her forehead. "Do you remember what I said?"

"You said you've got me."

I smile at her breathy tone as she repeats my words.

"I do. If you don't evolve fully, then I've got you, Vivie. We'll leave if we have to, go into hiding. No one will take you from me."

Our gazes hold in a moment of silence. She sees clear through me —through the layers of walls I've built around a heart that's never known love—and touches the very core of who I am. *I am hers.* I stroke her cheek. *And she is mine.*

"Hey, I was thinking." She tips her head back against the door and bats her pretty lashes. "How would you like to be my prom date?"

"I thought we weren't making plans." I tried asking her about prom a month ago when the posters began popping up in the halls at school. She refused to plan. She wanted to wait until after my birthday.

Her arms tighten around my back. "I changed my mind. Let's make plans. If we make plans, it means everything is going to work out."

"Everything *is* going to work out," I promise as my mouth descends on hers. We kiss until Elias shouts our names, then I kiss her some more. Memorizing the shape and feel of her lips beneath mine. The satin of the skin at the back of her neck. The ginger smell of her hair. "I love you, Vivie," I tell her, before I walk her outside and watch her drive away with Elias.

RISE

VIVIENNE

I'm blindfolded and sitting in the middle of a ritual circle in the wilderness alone. Well, not alone—with witches. Real witches. Oh, at night. Because it wouldn't be scary enough without adding the nocturnal animal sounds. A twig snaps to my right, and I jerk to the left, nearly toppling over. *Get a grip, Viv.* Murmurs reach my ears. Are they doing the spell now? I pull my knees closer to my chest. Addie said to sit here and be still. And no matter what, I'm to keep my mouth shut. Message received.

The steady rush of the waterfalls in the distance gives me a slight reference point for my location. Finally, when I'm unsure if I can take another minute in the dark, goosebumps tease my arms as the snow-muted crunch of footsteps approaches. There's a dim glow through the dark blindfold I wear. Candles? They're witches; surely that's it. A bitter aroma permeates the air, burning my nose, as voices chant. No introductions then? Okay.

"Lie back, Vivienne," someone says.

I do as they say but my mind can't stop wondering who these women are. Cressida is a nymph, the Kasuns are shifters, Jack Peters is a hellhound. Which of my classmates are witches? *Rose Howe!* Is Scarlet Howe a witch like her mother?

Little they say or do makes sense to me. Where's Elias? He blindfolded me the moment we were out of Breckin's sight, saying it was a requirement of the witches. I tried following along with his turns as we drove, but it was impossible. We weren't on the road long and the falls are near, so we're either off a street in Havenwood Heights or off Alverson Road. Addie met us when we got out of the truck and walked us through the grass and woods before telling Elias he'd come far enough. He'd pumped my hand for courage, then let go, allowing Addie to guide me the rest of the way.

A cool hand takes mine, and I flinch when something sharp pricks my finger. Addie warned me beforehand, but it doesn't lessen the shock.

"Sanguinem dimittere eam."

"Ea sanguis revelare."

"Revelare in sanguine suo."

A sharp pang hits my chest and spreads through my torso as my limbs twitch uncontrollably. The voices continue.

"Potestatem dimittere."

"Angelus revelare."

"Virtutem revelare."

Behind the words I can't understand are more chants. Constant and musical, the soft words lull me into relaxation, even as the pain in my chest grows. My back arches off the frozen ground as my spine pops. I bite my lip and suck in air. The chanting accelerates, becoming louder. Phrases like "light of the moon" and "power of the sisterhood" reach my ears, and I focus on them, instead of the inferno igniting my skin.

I grit my teeth. My ears pop, and a million sounds infiltrate my senses. And still the fire burns.

I slap the ground with my hands, searching for something to hang onto as the taste of the air coats my tongue and the aroma of the forest overwhelms my nose. And still the fire burns.

Writhing at the heat, I curl into a ball on my side. The witches' chants no longer reach me. My mind is focused on one thing, and that's the undeniable need to escape.

My hands long to claw at my skin. I want to rip open my chest and flee. I want to go home. I want to . . . I scream and kick at the ground.

Fight it, angel.

The voice is so clear, so divine, I still as tears fill my eyes.

Fight the darkness.

"Custodire a malo suo."

I thrash on the ground, curling into myself more when Breckin's scent hits me. He's on my coat and in my hair. Snow and pine. I inhale deeply and see his face. Breckin's words fill my head as a growl competes with his voice. A cold sensation trickles up my spine and over my shoulder, dousing the fire burning my insides.

The witches stop chanting.

"Custodire a malo suo," the main voice stands out once more. She repeats the phrase twice more. I whimper and fall into darkness.

"Vivienne?" I jerk at Elias's voice. "Viv?"

Heat washes over me as I open my eyes and look to the right. Elias stands in the open door of his truck, watching me. My breathing hitches. I'm in his truck. How did I get in his truck?

"Shhh." He cups the side of my head, my wet hair clinging to my face.

"What?" I ask on a shaky breath. "Where's Addie? What happened?"

"How do you feel?"

I blink once more, then shake my head. "I'm . . ."

A knife slashes through my chest, and I turn, gripping the dashboard as an agonizing feeling of brokenness invades my soul.

"Breckin," I gasp, black spots filling my vision.

Elias chuckles lightly and touches my arm. "Of course, let's go home." His face morphs from one to two, and I sway in my seat. His grin disappears. "Viv?"

A crunch so sickeningly painful and gloriously satisfying all at once fills my mind. The scent of smoldering embers fills my nostrils. "Oh, God . . . something's wrong, Elias."

Vivie!

His voice is as real as my own, and when he screams, I'm thrown forward, slamming my head into the dash, as my back is torn apart by a pair of wings.

Elias curses, catching me as I tumble from his truck and stumble forward. "What the . . . I have . . . those are . . ." I grab his arms for balance. My shock at having wings is crippled by the terror coursing through my veins. "Breckin?"

Vomit rises in my throat.

Elias steadies me. "What is it?"

"He's . . . he screamed. There was a horrible sound." The wings in my back toss about frantically. Elias's fingers dig into my skin as I straighten. "I'm gonna be sick," I manage on a gasp as the fracture of bones reverberates through my mind. My gut churns, though somewhere within me there's an odd rejoicing at the pain.

A light illuminates the darkness, and it takes a moment for my mind to process that it's coming from Elias's cellphone.

"Can you control those?" he asks as he shuffles me back toward his truck.

"Control them?" *Is he kidding me? I have freaking wings.* The beat of a bug's wings tickles my ear. My tongue catches the taste of the spray in the air from the falls. My angelic abilities are working at full speed. The dizziness comes in waves, ebbing and flowing through my body. Through the cell, I hear Breckin's voicemail pick up, and my wings go berserk again.

"He would have answered," Elias says, pocketing the phone and looking around. His head tips to the sky.

"Elias!" A shout comes out of the black night sky.

"Hamon," Elias mutters low. He grabs me and pushes me back, his body blocking mine a moment before Breckin's father lands.

"Are you two okay?" Hamon asks. In his hand is the glowing sword he used to end Zeke. "They have Breckin. The house was ransacked. He's here . . . I smell him."

A sudden anger invades my being, and Hamon's face snaps in my direction. His blue eyes narrow, and the sword wavers.

"Hamon, it's all right. It's her. It's Vivienne." Elias speaks in the voice of an adult soothing a child. He holds one arm in front of him while the other holds me tucked behind him. "He's not here."

Nothing Elias says makes sense. *Who's not here? Who's he?* I push at Elias, surprised when my strength moves his arm.

"Who has Breckin? What happened? My mother was at the house! Is she okay?" I toss the questions at Hamon as I unsteadily step out of Elias's shadow.

"Viv," Elias's warning halts my steps.

Hamon's face is at once handsome elegance and righteous fury. My gaze flicks to his fist wrapped tight around the hilt of the glowing angel blade, and my jaw tightens. His knuckles flex and relax while he watches every move I make. Somewhere within, an old sadness surfaces, and my throat tightens. *Is that Phaedra's blood?* My head whirls.

"Hamon, put the sword away," Elias says in that same warning tone.

Hamon looks between us. His eyes touch on every part of me, from my shoes to the tips of my new wings. The perusal stirs up the flame of rage inside my chest. Rage and sadness—the two are at war within me. A broken sob escapes my lips.

"I can feel them." I clutch Elias's shoulder and turn him to face me. "Phaedra's blood and my father's—it's like two creatures sharing my body. Is that normal? They're in my head, in my chest."

With a pleading look at Hamon, Elias takes my hand. "You'll learn to control them. I promise. I'll help you," he says.

"It worked, then. Her mother had her blood bound?" The angel blade disappears behind Hamon's wings before he steps forward. My body fights to both step closer and move farther away from him. "How did she know?" Hamon asks Elias as his eyes search my face.

"I don't think she did. She went to a friend, who took her to the Court. A member of the coven told her he was damned, but I don't think she knew who he was."

Hamon throws his head back.

"Is this your idea of divine intervention?" he shouts angrily at the sky.

"Are you talking about my father? About . . . Sam?" It takes me a moment to remember the name of the angel who fathered me. "Did you know him?"

"Know him?" Hamon spits the words out in a growl, and my muscles tense. I want to punch him. *Why do I want to punch Breckin's father? What is wrong with me?*

"Vivienne, your father—"

"Your father betrayed Heaven. He betrayed us. He is the reason Phaedra was killed," Hamon interrupts Elias. "He's the reason Breckin has remained hidden all these years."

My head shakes as bile once again burns the back of my throat.

"Your father has your soul mate, Vivienne. And I don't think he plans on giving him back."

JOURNEY (READY TO FLY)

VIVIENNE

"That's enough, Hamon," Elias says through clenched teeth. "What her father did back then isn't our main concern right now. Rachel was at the house. Did you see her?"

"I didn't go in. I saw the shattered glass, then I caught *his* scent." He jerks his chin my way. "I followed it."

My legs carry me forward, away from Elias and Hamon as they argue back and forth. Mom has to be all right. I would know if she wasn't. *Wouldn't I?* I clench my eyes closed and beg for her safety as Hamon's accusations overwhelm me. *My father took Breckin? He betrayed the angels behind me, killed Phaedra?* All these connections between my family and Breckin's—it's part of the plan . . .

"In human terms, it means we were matched to fulfill our destiny."

"Destiny?"

"C'mon, Viv. Don't tell me you don't believe in destiny? That people are put in places to make things happen, or sometimes bad things happen to good people because they need to learn a lesson that will bring them to something better?"

"I don't know what I believe in. Maybe things happen for a reason. Maybe it's coincidence."

"We're not a coincidence, Vivie."

Drawing a deep breath, I ask over my shoulder, "Where is he?"

Elias and Hamon are studying me when I turn around. What a sight I must be, with my half-shredded shirt, damp hair, and disobedient black wings. I roll my shoulders back and stretch my tiny frame taller.

"Where would he take Breckin?" I ask Hamon.

A cold mask slams down over Hamon's eyes. "That is not your concern. I will deal with it."

I ignore his refusal. "Elias?"

Hamon takes one step my way, his wings expanding to their full size. The white trim around the feathers glows in the darkness. "Did you not hear what I said, daughter of Andras? I will find my son."

Living in Colorado, we're taught that most predators will not attack unless provoked. There are many sayings—don't poke the bear, let sleeping dogs lie—it's common sense. Hamon just poked the bear. My hands shake as the fuse to a frenzy of emotions ignites. *Be still,* I order the wings dancing at my spine. They listen and snap back at attention. Taking three steps forward, I move into Hamon's personal space. His presence has the two halves within me at war. I better understand my internal conflict now. The desire to hurt versus the desire to comfort. Andras, his enemy, and Phaedra, his . . . what? What was she to Hamon? Judging by the pain written on his face when he mentioned her being killed—I would say she was his love.

I catch Elias's subtle move forward as I sniff. "I am the daughter of Rachel Freeman. I am a daughter of Phaedra. I am not the daughter of Andras. I will never be his daughter. If he is who you say . . . if he has Breckin, he is nothing to me. And if you think you can order me away from *my soul mate,* you are mistaken." My voice shakes, and I ball my hands into fists. "I may be tiny, but I am not useless. Help me find him, Hamon."

Elias speaks up. "Viv, you can't fight. You're not strong—"

I suck in a breath, ready to argue, but Hamon speaks first. "No," he says with a half smile. "Breckin is her mate. She's right. She can be of help."

"Breckin wouldn't want her involved."

"And I wouldn't forgive myself, or you, if something happened to him, and I wasn't involved." I focus on Hamon, sensing his agreement. "I felt his pain. I will feel it again, and when I do, I will follow after him. If you know where to find him, you'll save us the headache, and my bond with him may help us."

"They'd take him to Amartía."

My dark side, my father's blood, leaps at the word. *Uh-mar-tea-uh*, I pronounce the word mentally, and the darkness jolts again. Muted shouts echo at the outer reaches of my mind. A searing pain burns through my shoulder, and I scream out loud. Elias grabs for me, and my wings slap him away. He reaches a second time, and the appendage slaps him again.

"They're hurting Breckin," I say between shallow breaths. "He's being—" Another bone shatters, and a low guttural sound rips at my heart.

"Elias, you need to go to the house and find Rachel. Make sure she is all right and see if they left anything. Vivienne and I will head for the nearest tomb and await your call."

"You're going to need me, Hamon. You can't go down there without backup."

"I have backup." He points to me. "And you've lost enough."

"Hamon . . ."

"Don't argue with me. Stay here. More of the damned could come in search of Breckin. Or Vivienne, if she was the one they were after. You need to alert the Court and maybe call in a few favors to keep things safe here, but don't come after us. This isn't their war, Elias. This is ours."

Breckin's agony has faded to a dull throb in my mind as Hamon wraps an arm around my waist and pulls me close, pressing my cheek to his chest. My wings don't fight his touch as they brush his forearm, but I'm too spent to care.

"I can't fly with you any other way with your wings like that," Hamon apologizes.

"Just get me to Breckin. That is all I care about."

We shoot high above Havenwood Falls, then hover there amongst the hanging clouds. "Can you tuck your wings close to your body?"

"I don't know." All the times Elias and Breckin worked with me on pulling my abilities out of my body—they never told me how to put them away.

"You breathe, Vivienne. It's an order from your mind. It's not difficult."

"Says the man born this way," I grumble as Hamon's eyes widen.

"Vivienne, it was in a fight with Andras and his army that Elias had his wings irreparably ripped from his back. Do you want to get to Breckin, or not?"

My stomach roils at the picture of Breckin's beautiful ebony and amber wings laying discarded and bloody on the ground. Inhaling deeply through my nose, I close my eyes and focus on my wings' movement. I search for the strand of control, the fiber connecting my wings to my brain. When I sense a line of energy moving, I follow it, riding it like a wave until I'm in the middle of my wings. It's an odd sensation. Like I can see down to the molecular level of my being. The luminescent outline of ebony wings, like Breckin's, and yet different. They're dainty, smaller at the base, tilting up like the letter V, before jutting out near my shoulders and angling toward the sky. Mentally I reach for the edge of my left wing and pull it toward my body. Then I reach for the right.

"Good job," Hamon says before he takes off at high speed.

Flying as an angel isn't the same as flying as a human. Hamon moves at twice the speed that Breckin ever did, and yet it feels like everything is passing slower. The wind rushes over my head and body, rustling my wings—which have miraculously stayed close—and jostling my legs about. I focus on my body, willing every muscle to remain still. It's surprisingly easy, and somehow my usual fears of heights and falling is gone.

"Will you tell me about Phaedra?" I ask after a few minutes of flight.

Hamon rolls his neck but he doesn't answer.

"Will you tell me about Andras then?"

Still no answer.

"Do you want to save your son, or get revenge?"

He gives a low harrumph. "Can't I have both?"

I sure hope so, but . . . "What if you can't?"

What if there's only one option here? From every hint that Elias has tried to put down about Hamon, I feel as though I know his answer, but I don't want to be wrong. Breckin is my only choice. He needs to be Hamon's, too.

"Vivienne—"

"You can call me Viv," I interrupt. "Vivienne is a mouthful, and no one uses it."

We bank left, and I draw in a breath.

"Very well, Viv." The nickname is strange on his lips. There's something so formal about his enunciation. "My entire existence on earth has been about finding Andras and ending him."

The control on my wings slips, and we deviate from our course. The minor break in our aerodynamics causes turbulence, and Hamon's arm tightens as he slows. I draw my wings back into my spine with a curse and an apology. We level out, then dip toward the ground. The city below us is covered in lights. We circle the city before dropping lower.

The moment we land, I push away from him and look around. A cemetery? The lights of the city are miles away but easy to see. We're in Denver. In a cemetery. What is this Amartía place? Hamon said we'd go to the nearest tomb . . .

"Anything?"

I spin around, expecting Hamon to be speaking to me, but he's on his phone. *Elias! Mom!*

"She's fine." Hamon sighs into the phone as his gaze keeps constant watch over our surroundings. "Elias wants to speak with you." He holds out the phone, and I eagerly snatch it from his hand.

"Elias? Is my mom—"

"She's fine, Viv. She's here. Breckin hid her."

"Can I speak with her?" My grip tightens on the cell phone as their voices mingle through the line.

"Viv, sweetie?"

"Mom!" Tears flood my eyes, and I blink them back. I will not show Hamon my tears. "What happened?"

"I'm fine, hon. We were silently watching television when Breckin jumped up. He ordered me to go through the doorway in the game room and lock myself in the safe room. I didn't hear a thing until Elias showed up. I didn't know he was gone. I'm sorry. I should have made him come with me."

"No, no . . . it's not your fault." It's just like him to run into the fight instead of hide from it. "I hope you know why I had to go with Hamon, though. I need to help find him, Mom."

"I know." Her voice is filled with emotion. "Please be careful, Viv. I love you."

"I love you, too."

The phone is shuffled, then Elias returns. "Viv?"

"Yeah?"

"Trust Hamon, okay?"

I glance over my shoulder at Breckin's father. They look more like brothers than father and son. It's a bit disconcerting. As is the sadness I feel every time I look at him. The bitterness that accompanies my sadness isn't so bad. I can work with that side of my blood right now. "Are you sure?"

"Breckin is like a son to me, Viv. I would not have let Hamon take you and go after him if I was not sure. Trust him."

Trust the man who hurt my angel. I'll try.

We hang up, and Hamon faces me. He shoves his hands into his pockets and cocks his head to one side. He probably heard everything we said. Good. Let him know I don't trust him.

"I will not let you use Breckin for revenge," I say as I slap his phone into his chest. He yanks his hand from his pocket and takes the phone.

"I have no intention of using Breckin for revenge," he says as his other hand wraps around my wrist. "I plan on using you for revenge."

BREATH

BRECKIN

*A*martía. Elias told me about the home of the more dangerous fallen and damned when I was younger. An underground world where the wicked come to play. The only playing I've witnessed is the playing they've done with me. Every bone in my body has been snapped twice since they found me at the house. The feathers from my wings are scattered about the floor in the dark cavern they've kept me in. The healing process is agonizing. The slow repair of each hairline crack in my bones drains my energy.

They know how to keep me down.

They mention Hamon's name, so I lay here and I wait for him, knowing that is why I was taken captive.

I also wait for Vivienne, because the moment I arrived, I knew.

The vision I had—the one with her screams in the pitch black and the scent of ashes—that vision happens here.

FIGHT ON

VIVIENNE

*M*y body tenses, and my wings shoot out. Is he betraying me, the daughter of his enemy, to save his son? I can't fault him. What wouldn't I do to save Breckin?

Hamon takes a step closer, and I stand my ground. I will not cower before him.

"He's here," Hamon says. I arch a brow and search our surroundings. "Your father, Vivienne. He will be down there, in Amartía. Since word of my involvement with a Nephilim in Havenwood Falls spread, he's had the damned ones looking for answers."

"Zeke?" I ask.

"And others."

"So, what? You're going to hand me over in exchange for Breckin?"

His careless shrug stings. Not that I expected much out of him, but he did save my life, twice. Why bother if I meant nothing to him? A rising panic presses in.

"Breckin won't let you do that. He won't leave me with the damned."

"Not merely the damned. Your father. And I doubt Breckin is in much of a position to fight it, Viv." He looks from side to side, then jerks his head toward the left. "This way. Let's go."

Even if I could fly on my own, I wouldn't fly away. I need to get to Breckin, and Hamon is my ticket in. So I follow.

It's dark, but it's easy to ascertain the age of the cemetery. We pass crumbling monuments and tombs with every step. The air is ripe with a rusty soil scent. In the distance, a statue rises above the rest, an angel with its wings silhouetted by the moon. I keep my eyes on the angel until we've passed by.

"Tell me the story about Phaedra." He doesn't reply. "You refuse, Elias refused, my mother refused. It must be one heck of a story if no one will tell it."

He inhales sharply. "It doesn't matter."

That draws a laugh from me. "Doesn't matter? Isn't that why we're all here?"

He stops, and his eyes glow in the moonlight as he looks at me. *That's right. I do know a little about the past.*

Walking again, he sighs. "There were four of us. Me, Elias, Phaedra, and Andras. Angels were created to be companions, much like humans were created. We weren't made to bond with one another, but after a while Andras, Elias, and I became true brothers. And Phaedra was loved by us all."

"Loved?" I ask. Romantically? Or platonically? The pain I've picked up in their voices when they mention her lead me to believe there is at least some of the former.

"She tolerated us. We were cocky angels who constantly competed to be the best. You wouldn't know it, but Elias is ridiculously competitive. Phaedra kept us from finding too much trouble."

"I always thought the whole point of angels was worshiping God."

He huffs. "Sort of. We've existed for eons. We do not count the passage of time as humans do. I couldn't tell you how long I've been on earth, let alone in existence. The Creator's intent changed when He created man. Angels were given free will, same as humans, but until man was born, we did not find a need to express it."

I can't stop the awe from creeping in as I look at Hamon. I'm talking to an angel who lived in the heavens. I've never dug into my religious beliefs. A higher power, sure, but what all that entails . . . I'm still uncertain. Or I was, until Breckin flew into my life.

"The four of us were assigned as lords over Creation. Dominions. Our job was to oversee the tasks of other angels. Andras grew bored of that task. The more we watched mankind exercise their free will, the more jealous he became. Many angels felt the same. We watched as man sinned again and again and were forgiven. It did not seem like justice."

"And that was when the heavenly wars began?" I ask, knowing some of the concepts of the Fall from art and reading.

"Yes. Like wars on earth, it was monstrous. Brothers and sisters fought one another. I was forced to end the existence of angels I'd known my entire life. Andras fell with the others, pushed out by the Creator, forbidden from ever returning."

Hamon's words hang in the air between us as we turn down a path going deeper into the cemetery. A grassy knoll rises to our left, and built into the knoll are a line of crypts. We stop before the third one. A surge of elation rises within my chest coupled with a sinking fear. The air is thicker here, dense with a blanket of despair. My wings pull tightly against my spine, as though they fear this place.

I study the crypt made with large stones and an arched door. A name is carved across the top, but years' worth of lichens and moss obscure it.

"What is this?" I step closer to the black iron double doors.

"The way to Amartía."

"A crypt? In a public cemetery?" That can't be safe.

"Only those without loyalties to Heaven can enter unexpected."

"But then . . . how do I get in?"

Hamon moves to my side and wraps a hand around the gate.

"You have his blood, Viv," Hamon says as he tugs the gate open.

Swallowing my fear, I enter the crypt on shaky legs. There's nothing to see in the pitch of night. My angel vision allows for outlines of walls and a black door before us. Hamon waves his hand, motioning me forward, so I go. An unfamiliar symbol consisting of lines and circles is etched into a piece in the center of the iron door.

"The mark of Amartía. The mark of the damned."

Hamon touches the mark, and the door clicks, then swings open.

"So you *are* damned then?"

He flashes a small grin. "No, I am expected."

If I had to imagine the scent of Hell, this would be it. Smoke and ash billow out from the entrance. Red embers litter the path before us.

"Go in, Vivienne," Hamon says, leaning over my back.

My wings wrap around my shoulders at his nearness. "You don't have to do this, Hamon."

"Do what?" He nudges me in the side, and I cross the threshold.

"Don't turn me over to him. Breckin will never forgive you."

"I'm not in the business of buying my son's forgiveness."

Biting my lip, I walk forward until I stumble down a step. My hand touches the steaming wall, an ember burning my skin.

"Amartía isn't a fixed place. There's dark magic at work here. If you were to enter from another crypt, you might find yourself in a garden, or a mansion."

But we get a black cave of fire and brimstone? Lovely. I take the steps carefully, going deeper and deeper underground. A breeze passes by, and I can almost imagine the scent of pine and snow. It makes my chest ache. His painful scream haunts me, and I grasp onto anything to keep from fixating on what he may be going through.

"So, Andras fell, then Phaedra fell, too?"

"Fell? Phaedra? Never in a million years would she fall from grace. Phaedra refused to believe that Andras couldn't be brought back around. He'd been led astray by consummate liars, turned by the master of deception. She swore she could make him see the error in their ways."

I come to a stop at the bottom of the staircase and wait for Hamon's direction. There are two paths. One glows with light at the end of a long stone-and-root hallway; the other is like the path we've just come down—embers and darkness. A smile trembles on his lips.

"That way," he says smoothly, pointing me toward the darkness and fire.

"She had a soft heart." I speak my thoughts out loud, and Hamon grunts.

"She did. She left without telling us. She just disappeared."

To save her friend. Elias hoped my soft heart would save Breckin and Hamon. That I would be their path to redemption. But how?

"So you left Heaven to go after her?" *Because we loved her more than we loved Him,* Elias had said.

"We did, but time on earth moves differently than in Heaven, and when we found her, Andras was long gone. She was heartbroken and would never tell us what happened—only that he refused her offers to return."

How painful that must have been. For all of them. They left Heaven to save their friend, and look what happened.

"Elias and I were punished for leaving without permission. When we attempted to return to Heaven, we were locked out. Elias has waited for the call to return home all this time."

"Elias, but not you? Because you align yourself with Hell and don't expect to return to Heaven?" The question is bold.

"I lost my faith. I've wandered, but I do not align with Hell. I align with Elias."

I clutch my stomach as it dances. We must be close. "Why did you lose your faith?"

"Do you ask this many questions of my son?" He sounds as though he admires me. As quickly as I think it, I brush the thought away. If he admired me, we'd be doing this differently right now. I don't reply.

"Phaedra could never let go of the idea that Andras would come home, and I could never let go of my anger at his turning. I parted ways with Elias and Phaedra. I always came back, but never for long. It was while I was away, near the end of the 1800s, that Phaedra was stripped of her grace. Without her wings or any abilities, she settled into a near-human life in Havenwood Falls. After that, Elias and I took turns watching over her and fighting those who threatened us . . ." He stops speaking and pushes in front of me.

"And then what happened?"

Hamon rounds a corner, and his hand shoots back and wraps around my arm as burnt embers flutter by my face.

"Then he came home and found his best friend had lost his wings and his one true love had met an untimely death," says a voice in the distance.

A snap resounds as darkness becomes light, and in the middle of a cavern filled with black stalactite is an angel with dark curls and perfect olive skin. His wings are shades of blue, purple, and black, like Mom described. This is my father. Andras. At his feet, with one wing hanging at an odd angle and covered in blood, both fresh and dried, is Breckin.

Hamon has to physically restrain me as my wings stretch wide. I am fury. Every atom in my body that makes me human fights to get to Breckin. His name is a broken scream so loud, there's no doubt the rest of the fallen and damned know we're here. Breckin's wings spasm against the ground. They cover him like a blanket, protecting him, but the discoloration and blood covering his skin tells me they aren't enough.

"Careful," Hamon whispers against my ear as he holds me.

Andras tips his head back, his pale blue eyes closing halfway, as he takes a long whiff of the air. My insides go cold. "Very smart, my brother, using my daughter to find me."

"I am not your daughter." I buck at Hamon, my head slamming into his jaw. "Let me go."

Hamon's fingers dig into my arm. His hold is like steel bands trapping me to his side. I scream and fight, but he does not budge. "He will shred you to pieces and not give a single damn, Viv. Bide your time."

I settle, if only because fighting does me no good, and take deep breaths.

"I figured it was only fair, *brother*, since you have my son, that I return the favor." We step farther into the cave. "Do you notice anything about her? Anything familiar?"

Hamon pushes me forward, and I fall to my knees, still unaccustomed to the weight of my wings on my frame. Twenty feet away, Breckin shifts, and I'm hit with a wave of emotions and thoughts like a hammer to the head. I gasp, curling into a ball on my hands and knees as my stomach turns.

"She's Phaedra's?" Andras asks.

"She is. Her gene was so hidden in her line, it wasn't detectable. Not until my son woke it up."

The cavern shakes with Andras's laughter, and I lift my head so I can follow their conversation, wincing at the barrage of feelings Breckin sends my way.

Hamon has moved closer, closing the gap between himself and Andras. They're both standing at ease, as though this is a normal conversation between two old friends. My gaze shifts to Breckin's prone form once more.

Breck? Can you hear me? I'm getting you out of here.

If he hears the thoughts I'm projecting his way, he doesn't comment.

"So the Creator saw fit to give me a daughter of Phaedra's?"

"No. The Creator saw fit to give my son a daughter of Phaedra's," Hamon counters. His arm goes behind his back, and he reaches for his angel blade.

My muscles go taut, and I push up from my hands to kneel, ready to run for Breckin.

"Do you think I did not plan for you to show up?" Andras asks, and a door slides open on the wall behind him. Two of the damned appear. I recognize the one from that day at the park immediately. Cropped blond hair, brown wings. He smiles at me as he walks to Breckin's side. The other is dark like Andras, with spotted wings.

"Do you want to do this, Hamon? You could join us. You've lived on the edge for so long. He will not call you home."

"I have wanted nothing more than to avenge her death, Andras. Whatever happens to me doesn't matter . . . as long as you're gone."

Hamon hurls himself into the air and straight for Andras with a warrior's cry.

Vivie.

Breckin's voice snaps my attention back to where he lies. Beneath his wings, his head moves slightly, and his eyes appear just under their cover. I bite my tongue to keep from crying out as his golden gaze holds mine.

Those wings are sexy as hell.

My cry escapes, but Andras and Hamon's shouts cover the noise. The two hovering near Breckin are focused on the fighting and miss his movement.

Are you all right? I ask. His wing looks repaired. I dig around in my mind, searching for any pain he's having, and can't feel a thing.

Seeing you here has improved me vastly. Can you . . .

Breckin's thoughts turn to an audible shout as I'm thrown into the wall. My head smacks the ground, and everything goes hazy. Blinking rapidly, I use the stone wall to stand and take in the scene. Breckin is in a battle with both the dark and blond damned, while his father and Andras play cat and mouse.

"Do you know how surprised I was to find that you, who has always hated humans, had a son with one?" Andras drawls. "The reaper was happy to betray you and tell us of your son. The Nephilim with the human soul mate."

Hamon's low growl rumbles the cave. "The reaper paid for his greed with his existence."

"So I heard. I expected as much. You kept your son in hiding. You knew your enemies would go after him if they knew. And her—" Andras's gaze flicks to me. "What a lovely gift she is."

"You betrayed us," Hamon shouts.

"*He* betrayed us, Hamon. I left of my own free will."

"And took Phaedra with you. You knew she'd come after you, you knew she'd never give up, and you didn't care. She loved you enough to risk her salvation for yours."

"That was her choice."

They fly at each other at blinding speeds. The blade Hamon holds could end Andras's life with the right swipe, and I can't help but wonder if Hamon is choosing not to make that move. Then I see the smaller dagger in Andras's hand. The eerie blue is the same as the sword Hamon uses. Their fight is even.

A deep growl turns my head back to Breckin, and I run for him as he flings himself around the dark one and twists his body. Bones crack, and a knife falls to the ground. It doesn't glow, so it's not an angel blade, but it still draws blood.

"Breckin, watch out!" I warn as the blond grabs the knife and slices it across Breckin's rib cage. Breckin falters for a moment too long, and the blond's arm goes up at the same time as the dark one rises to his feet once more. Knowing he can't fight two at once, I launch myself into the air and hurtle toward the blond, taking him to the ground.

"What's your name?" I ask through gritted teeth as the blond and I wrestle around on the ground.

He flips me easily, and my wings protest the weight as he pins my arms above my head. "Jarrod, little hellcat. Why, are you asking me on a date?"

"No, I just wanted to know the name of the one I'm about to kill."

His white smile falls, and I buck my hips, tossing him forward, rolling and flipping until he's beneath me. My elbow smashes into his face, a sickening crunch telling me his nose is broken. It buys me a moment, but it's not long enough, and I'm thrown to the side.

"Your wing, Viv," Hamon shouts. I turn his way as I roll away from the blond, and Hamon points at his side.

With his focus on me, Hamon barely has time to move when Andras comes behind him. Andras's blade catches his side, and he grunts but whirls around and lands a kick to Andras's legs. Everything happens so fast. As our fathers trade punches, Breckin falls to the ground when the dark one he fights bashes a rock into the back of his head. He rips at Breckin's wing, bending the bottom half until it snaps, and once again the pain invades my body.

"No!" I cry out as something smashes against my gut, and I bend forward from the force.

"Vivienne. That's your name, isn't it?" Jarrod asks as his fingers grasp my hair and yank my head back. He looks down on me, his pretty white smile so out of place in this violent, desolate cavern. I reach around, my hand going to my back where my wings meet my spine. "Such a pretty little half angel. I'm glad I know the name of the princess I get to break."

His face lowers to mine, his wicked grin reminiscent of Zeke's in that alley, and my body tenses as my hand closes in on what Hamon told me to look for.

"I am not a princess, Jarrod. Try to break me, and I'll avenge what is mine."

My arm swings around, and with all the strength of two angels and a girl who wants her soul mate and heart returned to her, the glowing dagger Hamon hid among my feathers slices across Jarrod's throat from ear to ear. Darkness pours from his throat, sending the former angel to the ground in a pile of ashes, and I gag at the sulfur scent burning my nose.

SUNRISE

BRECKIN

*a*shes hit my face, and I raise my head to the sight of Vivienne standing, a dagger twirling around her fingers.

"And what is your name, dark one?" she asks, looking my way, and the pressure at my back releases.

"This isn't my fight," the one I've been fighting says, raising his arms and backing away.

"Oh, I believe you made it your fight when you attacked what's mine."

Damn, the electricity that explodes every time I see her blows a fuse. Angel Vivie is badass.

The coward runs for the wall, disappearing through a doorway, and I grit my teeth, praying Vivienne doesn't follow. She watches the door for a moment longer than necessary before she finally turns to me, and her entire face changes.

Gone is the badass angel warrior with gleaming black wings.

"Hey," she says, falling to her knees and pulling my head into her lap. This is *my* Vivie. My delicate little human. "Are you all right? Can you heal yourself?"

Her hand skims over my wing. Her scowl and furrowed brow tell me it looks about as good as it feels. When she swipes at the liquid seeping from a cut over my eye, I take a deep breath.

"My avenging angel." I lift a hand and tangle my fingers in the ends of her hair dangling over my face.

"That's right. You awoke me. Now I get to avenge you." She smiles, and I groan as the crackling of my healing bones echoes between us. She flinches, and I know she can feel my pain. "It's okay, Breckin. I've got you. You're safe."

I blink, trying to keep my heavy eyes open. I get them both—the badass angel warrior and the delicate girl. For eternity.

"Watch out," Hamon shouts, and I turn in time to see Andras flying our way, an angel blade in his hand. Vivienne collapses on top of me, her dark wings covering us both as Hamon screams and bodies collide.

A whispered "I'm sorry, brother" reaches me before the scent of death and ash. Vivienne jerks up enough for me to see Hamon on his knees over what's left of her father before my eyes close.

I WAKE at home in the upstairs master suite with Vivienne tucked in at my side, one ebony wing covering me. Protecting me. Everything after seeing Andras fall is a blur. Vivienne and Hamon supported me as we hurried through the halls of Amartía and back to the cemetery. I have no memory of how we returned home.

I reach for Vivienne's wing and stroke the feathers. She lifts her face off my chest and smiles.

"You know you're supposed to put these things away occasionally."

Her lips purse. "If only I knew how."

I scratch at her feathers, and they shiver, making me smile as Vivienne releases a little groan. "I know all the right spots to scratch. I'll teach you if you're nice to me."

She shifts and rolls farther onto my chest so her wings spread out before me. "How nice?"

All the dirty thoughts run through my mind—and into hers—but they're interrupted by a knock on the door. "Breckin?"

The door opens. Vivienne slides to my side, her face red as I sit up, surprised to see him here. "You're still here."

Hamon looks between us. "I thought you both might like answers."

"Yeah, um . . . we'll be down in a minute."

He closes the door, and I glance out the window for the first time. It's daylight. "We're missing school, huh? It is Monday, isn't it?"

Vivienne climbs from the bed. "It is. Obviously, I can't go like this. We can miss a day or two after everything."

I throw on a shirt as I watch her move about the room. If I thought her beautiful before, it's nothing like what I feel now. She radiates so much light, I want to shield my eyes. And her wings . . .

"What happened with the Court?" I ask. I missed so much.

"They reversed the spell." She shrugs. "Elias sat me in his truck, then BAM, everything hit. The spell was like a belt, holding it all in, and once it was released, I gained access to it all. I don't even need sleep anymore."

"The one ability you really wanted." I wink. "But your father—"

"He wasn't my father, Breck. He was just a fallen angel who damned himself, then slept with my mom. I have no feelings toward him. Maybe I will someday, but he would have killed you out of spite."

I grab her hand as she moves to the door and pull her into my chest. "I'm still sorry."

Vivienne tucks her face against the side of my neck, and we stand that way for a long time.

WE CONGREGATE IN THE BASEMENT, because every meeting of importance happens in the basement. I tried not to look at the broken glass and shredded furniture on the first floor as I walked by. At least downstairs everything feels normal. Well, everything except for Hamon standing here, and Rachel, and Vivienne with her wings. I make a mental note to ask her how her mother dealt with seeing those for the first time.

As if watching television, a vision flicks through my mind of Rachel's shocked face as Vivienne returned with Hamon and me. I look at Vivienne leaning against the counter in the kitchen.

Wow. Your abilities have magnified, huh?

She tips her head and arches a brow. *Think of how much fun this will be.*

Trust me, Vivie, I'm making a list.

"How are you feeling?" Elias asks me as he takes a seat across from Rachel.

"One hundred percent." Hamon and Elias share looks of relief. "Andras liked to talk. He filled me in on who he was, who you all were. And he told me about Phaedra."

"Her story is all there in the journal." Elias points to the table. "We agreed you two should read it."

Hamon takes a deep breath. "Breckin, you should know that I never intended to turn you toward Hell. All these years, I've done what I had to do because I was searching for Andras. I hid you here with Elias and stayed away to keep you safe. I knew if he ever found out about you, he would come for you. My allegiance was never to Hell."

"So it was all lies then?"

"Yes, to protect you. To get into Amartía. To find where Andras was, and to keep other angels, fallen or damned, away. If they feared me, they'd stay away from you." He grips the back of a chair and takes a deep breath. "I made things difficult on you because I needed you to be as strong as you could be when the inevitable happened. The last few months, things unraveled. The more ambitious of the fallen followed me everywhere once they caught wind of Vivienne's existence —thanks to Sebastian. The human with an angel soul mate was a huge draw for the dark side."

"Is the only reason you agreed to save her from Sebastian because she was a descendent of Phaedra's?" I ask.

"No. I had no idea who your soul mate was. When I spoke to Elias, he didn't say her name. I knew who Vivienne was, as a person, but I didn't know she was yours." I'm skeptical, and he senses it. "I saved her for you, Breckin. I know what it is to lose the person you love."

"Were you and Phaedra a couple, then?" Vivienne asks, straightening from her spot leaning on the counter.

"I loved her enough to make her mine, but she couldn't stop feeling guilty."

"For what?"

"She could never forgive herself for causing me and Elias to leave Heaven. Just like with Andras, her concern was our salvation."

Vivienne crosses the room and touches Hamon's shoulder. "You have to forgive yourself." He draws back. "I didn't read the journal, but my mother told me about it. Phaedra wrote a lot about you and your quest to find Andras. Elias alluded to the same. You are not to blame for her death. She chose to stay here because she loved you two. That was her choice."

Hamon's finger grazes Vivienne's cheek, his eyes softer than I've ever seen them. "I'm sorry I scared you last night."

Scared her? My back prickles to attention. "How did you scare her?"

Vivienne laughs. "Your son is a little overprotective, if you haven't noticed," she says as she holds her hand out for me to take. "I may have told your father I would not let him use you for revenge. And he may have said something about using me instead."

I breathe through my nose and will my wings to remain away.

"It was the only way to find him. Amartía allows angels with undefined loyalties in, but the dark magic makes it like a labyrinth. The only doors open to you are the ones they want open. I've always had one—"

"The long hall with the light at the end?" Vivienne asks.

"Yes. You opened the other. The hall that led us to Andras. I used you to get my revenge."

Elias had tried to tell me to talk to Hamon, that he wasn't what I thought he was. In five months our lives, both Vivienne's and mine, have become unrecognizable. Everything has changed.

"What now?" I ask, my gaze moving around the room. To the father who was never present, but always protected me. To the uncle who stayed loyal to his friend, even when it cost him dearly. To the woman who held secrets to protect her daughter from potential harm, and to the girl who lit my soul on fire. "What happens when my birthday comes?"

I'd lived with the idea that I would have to make a choice to serve Heaven or Hell on my eighteenth birthday. I expect the answer I've heard on numerous occasions, but instead Hamon looks to Elias. "We'll do whatever normal people do on birthdays."

Vivienne's eyes go wide.

"Does that mean you're staying in town?" My heart picks up speed, and Vivienne shushes me in my head.

"I'd like to remain and see my son graduate. If that's all right with you."

My words stick in my throat, so I nod.

"Have you ever had a chocolate cake, Hamon?" Vivienne asks. "We'll definitely need a chocolate cake for his birthday."

Rachel and Elias laugh as Hamon looks at my girl with a confused expression.

I give her hand a squeeze. "Chocolate on chocolate," I correct my sugar addict.

"Well, of course. Only the best for you."

VIVIENNE and I are tangled up together on the basement couch later that afternoon. Hamon and Elias went with Rachel to the apartment to help her pack. The Freeman girls will be moving in with me, as will my father. It's all in the interest of safety and sanity.

I look at Phaedra's journal sitting on the coffee table.

"Phaedra lost her grace because when she was called back to Heaven, she refused to go. She didn't go after Andras on her own. She was sent by God, on a mission. She was sent to redeem him. She could have returned and lived out her eternity in splendor, but she chose an uncertain future because she could not bear the thought of leaving Elias and Hamon." I'm thinking out loud, still putting the pieces of the past together.

Vivienne's wing flutters about, and I reach around to stroke it. She's like a kitten crawling up on my lap every time she wants to be petted. "I can't say I blame her," she says.

"I think that's why I found you," I say thoughtfully. She looks at me expectantly. "Phaedra was sent to redeem, and when she didn't go home as called, she was stripped of her powers, but she maintained her immortality. Why didn't the Creator just make her human? Be done with her? Why did your mother come across the one angel who was the downfall of her ancestor, and instead of walking away or being scared—she had his child? Why are we soul mates? There was a plan, Vivie. Our destiny."

"Perhaps," Vivienne says with a smile. "I guess we'll never know, unless we're called back."

Being called to Heaven. That's a possibility I haven't allowed myself to ponder. My fingers brush through her hair. "You're not mad or resentful, even a little, for what has happened since we met?" I ask.

"Not at all. I would rather have this adventure with you, wherever it takes us, and know I'm with the one I love, the one my soul loves, than live a normal life and never have the love we share."

I kiss the top of her head. "I love you, Vivie, but you know we won't get very far on that adventure if you don't put those wings away."

She props her chin on my chest and looks up at me. "You keep saying that, but you haven't told me how to do it."

"Well"—I shift her on top of me— "the key is to relax." My hands go to either side of her spine and run along the edge where the wings meet the skin.

"Will you help me with that?" she asks, sliding up my chest until we're face to face.

"It would be my pleasure." My lips land on hers, coaxing and teasing as my fingers play upon her skin.

With a sudden jerk, Vivienne gasps and slaps at my chest. "Breckin, that was too naughty of you."

I withdraw the mental image with a laugh. "Sorry, I told you we were gonna have some fun with that."

EPILOGUE

VIVIENNE

Aren't you glad we don't have to have graduation in the cemetery like Sun and Moon Academy? Breckin's thoughts make me giggle as I sit among my fellow Havenwood Falls High graduates on the football field.

What is with that, anyway? It's obviously related to the supes, right?
I wish I could see his face as he laughs within my mind. *Of course. They have all sorts of strange customs there.*

Mayor Stuart wraps up her speech—something about the world of possibilities open to us, but in a fit of boredom, Breckin has kept my mind occupied with thoughts the entire time, some of them totally inappropriate for the occasion. I'm still floored by how much he hates human traditions.

Not all of them, Vivie. I liked prom, he reminds me mentally.
Prom. Yeah, that he liked. Dressing in a tux, indulging Mom with picture after picture, enduring dancing and chatting with kids from school—all knowing what he had planned afterward. Candles, flowers, slow dancing in the moonlight away from prying eyes, and . . .

The clearing of Breckin's throat in my head is akin to ice water being thrown on me. *Are those appropriate thoughts at this time, Miss Freeman?*

I huff, *You brought it up first.*

He laughs, and I swear I hear the sound outside my head as well as within.

When Principal Friske begins calling names for us to receive our diplomas, I tune Breckin's suggestive musings out. One by one I watch as kids I've known my entire life walk across the stage for the last time as Havenwood Falls Dragons. In the short months since I learned of the supernatural side of this town I've identified a host of species. Gallad Augustine, a witch. Macy Blackstone, a witch hunter—who dates Gallad. Love *really* is complicated for those two.

Are you feeling nostalgic?

Get out of my head, Breckin Roberts! I look back at the rows of seniors behind me as my row stands and works its way toward the front.

I can't help it. You're projecting all these crazy emotions. Something like a caress floats across my mind.

His mental touch causes my wings to spasm. They're eager to stretch. I've learned to shelter the appendages, but they don't appreciate long periods of confinement. The first few weeks of school after they appeared were hell.

I'm sad, Breck. How many of my friends will leave town and not return?

Hey, it's the closing of this chapter, but we are about to write something even more amazing, Vivie. We have so much to look forward to.

After the party, I remind him sternly, thinking of the traditional graduating class bonfire and camping party by the river we're to attend tonight.

Yes, after the party. I'm only looking forward to it because I can't wait to roll town square.

Again, I giggle. *So, you're not looking forward to sleeping with me in a tent all alone after months of having our parents under the same roof watching our every move? You're more interested in throwing toilet paper into trees and bushes and making a complete mess of the square? Should I be worried?*

Ahhh, Vivie. You have no *idea how much I'm looking forward to sharing a sleeping bag with you tonight.* My wings twitch again, and heat sweeps my body as he continues his soft words in my head. *Even more, I'm ready to fly, aren't you?*

Ready to fly.

Breckin and I planned a getaway after graduation. Just us, endless flight, and the world. Surprisingly, it was Mom who was on board with the idea first. Hamon and Elias weren't exactly thrilled. Poor Breckin —those two are the most overprotective father figures I've ever seen. It's comical, considering our soul bond, to watch the eons-old angels lecture Breckin on gentlemanly behavior. Eventually, with Mom's help, they came around. We're still unsure where our purpose lies. Hamon has switched his own purpose from avenging Phaedra to helping us figure out ours. If there is something we're meant to do, a reason for our bond, he'll figure it out. Of course, maybe we're supposed to live as normally as possible—go to college, get married, have a family one day. We'll discover our purpose, but right now, it's one day at a time.

"Vivienne Jane Freeman." Principal Friske calls my name, and I step onto the stage. Out in the cheering crowd sits my family. Mom— the woman who raised me by herself, always knowing that I might become something *more*. Elias—who gave up his wings trying to protect Phaedra, and gave up his freedom to protect Breckin. Then there's Hamon. Living with him has been eye-opening. He's fierce and loyal, and has taught Breckin and me a wealth of knowledge about our angelic abilities.

I shake Friske's hand and, like my friends before me, turn to the crowd and give a little jig. I did it! I survived high school at Havenwood Falls High.

We survived. Breckin butts into my head. Pushy angel.

Our gazes lock as I come down the steps of the stage and find him near the back of the senior class. Zara sits not far behind him, and we share a smile before my focus returns to Breckin.

Am I ready to fly? Breck, we're gonna soar, I promise.

The amber in his eyes flashes. *You've got that right,* my *angel.* The resolve in his tone is as strong as mine.

We will soar. Two half-angel soul mates destined to be. Tomorrow is filled with uncertainty, but the unknown no longer fazes me. I have Breckin at my side. Our eternity starts today.

We hope you enjoyed this story in the Havenwood Falls High series of novellas featuring a variety of supernatural creatures. The series is a collaborative effort by multiple authors.

Havenwood Falls High books by Michele G. Miller:

Awaken the Soul
Avenge the Heart

You might also enjoy these books in the Havenwood Falls High series:

Fata Morgana by E.J. Fechenda
Forever Emeline by Katie M. John
Reclamation by AnnaLisa Grant
Avenoir by Daniele Lanzarotta
Curse the Night by R.K. Ryals

Stay up to date at www.HavenwoodFalls.com

MICHELE G. MILLER

ABOUT THE AUTHOR

Michele writes novels with fairytale love for everyday life. Romance is central to her plots, where the genres range from Coming of Age Fantasy and Realistic Fiction to New Adult Romantic Suspense. She is the author of the bestselling From the Wreckage series, a Havenwood Falls author, and co-writes the Paper Planes series with author Mindy Hayes. Mindy and Michele also write clean contemporary titles under the pen name Mindy Michele.

Having grown up in both the cold, quiet town of Topsham, Maine, and the steamy, Southern hospitality of Mobile, Alabama, Michele is something of an enigma. She is an avid Yankees fan, loves New England and being outdoors, and misses snow. However, she thinks Southern boys are hotter, Alabama football is the only REAL football out there, and sweet tea is the best thing this side of heaven and her children's laughter!

Her family, an amazing husband and three awesome kids, have planted their roots in the middle of Michele's two childhood homes, in Charlotte, North Carolina.

Website: http://www.michelegmillerbooks.com/
Email: authormichelegmiller@gmail.com
Facebook: https://www.facebook.com/AuthorMicheleGMiller
Twitter: https://twitter.com/chelemybelles
Pinterest: http://pinterest.com/chelemybelles/
Instagram: https://instagram.com/chelemybelles/

ACKNOWLEDGMENTS

I'm so grateful to the people who support me through the book process and life:

My husband and kids deal with me forgetting laundry, dinner, carpool, emails, and the list goes on. How they put up with me I'll never know!

My amazing crew of readers, bloggers, and friends on Facebook and "in real life" keep me sane. You make this solitary life a little less solitary, and a lot more lifelike.

My core reader group on Facebook, Mindy and Michele's M&M's: Thanks for being a sounding board when needed, book pimps when needed, and friends always.

To Jo Pettibone: Thank you for walking with me from day one with Viv and Breck and being the best Alpha a writer could have. You talked me off the ledge a few times with this one. I'm so lucky to have you!

To Mindy: Thanks for having patience with me, and allowing me to write Avenge the Heart while you tried to plot Loss in A Major. Co-writing isn't much fun when your co-writer is busy with other projects. I'm grateful you indulge me. xoxo

To the Havenwood Falls family: This group continues to grow, but their generosity, creativity, and enthusiasm for this project astounds me. I'm so lucky to be able to write, and collaborate, with these amazing creatives. Many of the characters and places I mention in both of my Havenwood Falls books were created by others in this amazing group.

More specifically, thanks to these ladies for creating and sharing your characters with Viv and Breckin in Avenge the Heart:

R.K. Ryals: Jack Peters and Cressida Manos

And of course, a final HUGE thank you to Kristie Cook for creating Havenwood Falls and making this all possible. A year into this journey, I am still in awe of your business savvy and ingenuity.

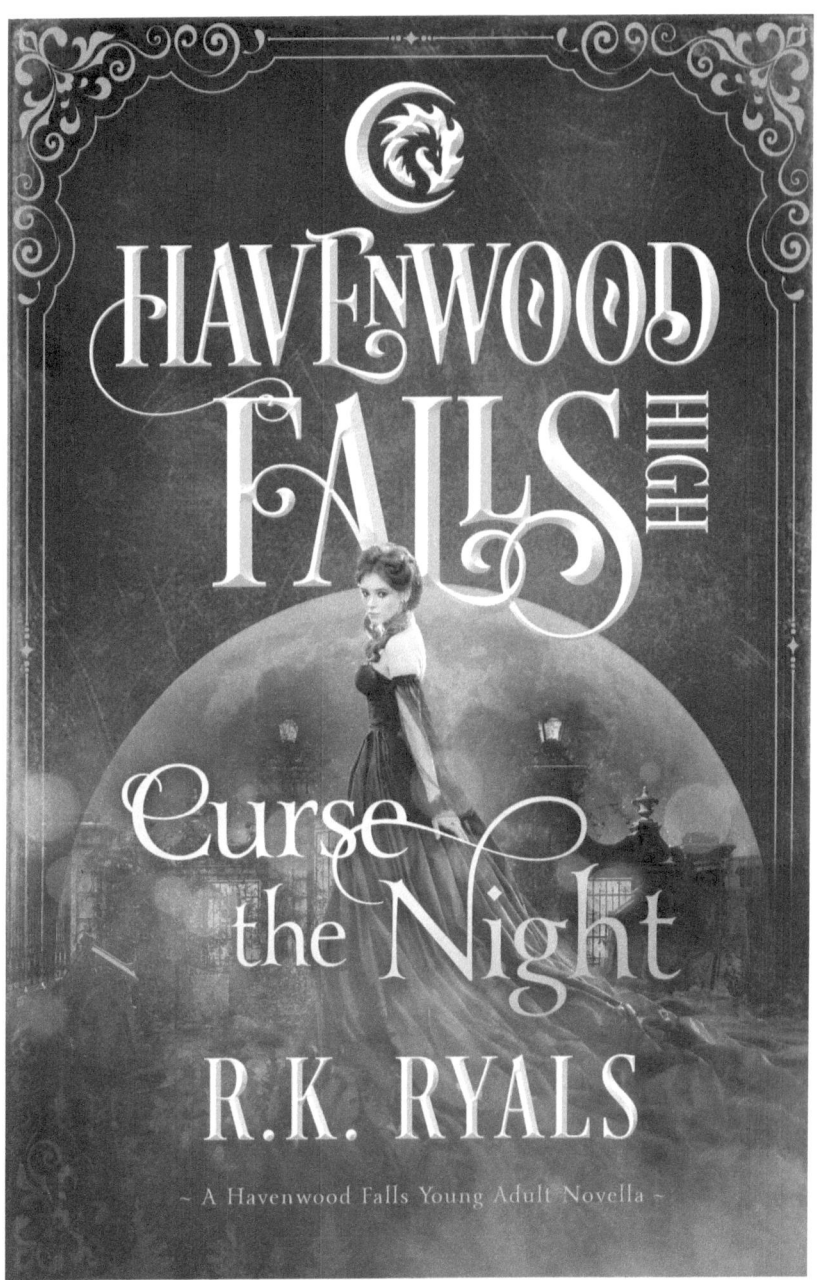

HAVENWOOD FALLS HIGH

Curse the Night

R.K. RYALS

~ A Havenwood Falls Young Adult Novella ~

Curse the Night (A Havenwood Falls High Novella) by R.K. Ryals

Jack Peters is everything a girl could want in a bad boy. Blunt, aloof, and ready to whisk you away on the back of his motorcycle. And that's just the way he likes it. Simple relationships. No commitment. High adrenaline. A shapeshifting Hellhound with a look that kills—literally—Jack hides behind his sunglasses and skulks in the cemeteries, biding his time until he's out of Havenwood Falls and on the road to bigger adventures.

He doesn't plan on Cressida Manos.

A seventeen year-old mountain nymph, Cressida has it all. A great family. A quiet life. And an annoying habit of being overly helpful and friendly with everyone. She's sunny, cheerful, dependable, and ... a vandal?

Caught on camera tagging buildings in the middle of the night, no one can believe Cressida Manos possible of malicious destruction of property. Especially Jack Peters, who stumbles on the redhead in the middle of graffitiing a tombstone.

Only Cressida doesn't remember her crimes, and the only one who believes she's innocent is the guy who caught her in the act.

CURSE THE NIGHT

AN EXCERPT

FIVE DAYS EARLIER . . .

"What is a four-letter word for 'being connected to someone'?" Paris asked, her pencil poised over the page of her open book, the front cover folded under the back. Light poured in through a large picture window overlooking Main Street, the glow highlighting the stained concrete flooring, light yellow walls, and multicolored display cases lining the interior of my family's art business, Apex Art Studio. It was early June in Havenwood Falls, the ease of summer already sinking into the bones, comfortable and unhurried. A peaceful respite before Midsummer's Night Terrors, a festival held in the square on the Summer Solstice.

Wet clay covered my hands, my fingers working the lump on the potter's wheel. I was responsible for the handmade pottery the customers painted—the pieces we didn't have shipped in—and I loved it. The entire creative process was soothing. Hypnotizing.

"Is that the only hint?" I asked, pressing my thumb into the center of the lump, my gaze flicking to the dark-haired, dark-skinned girl sitting cross-legged on the floor next to my stool.

Named after the place where her parents met and where she was conceived, my best friend Paris Francine Callahan was fascinated with

149

crossword puzzles and had been since the day we were introduced in elementary school. Paris was human—an important distinction in Havenwood Falls, where a substantial portion of the population was supernatural—and shy. Extremely shy. Even though she was stunning enough to grace the cover of Vogue. I was the plain one out of the two of us, all five foot one, redheaded, pale-skinned, button-nosed, freckled inch of me.

"One of a matched pair?" Paris added, reading. "Third letter is a T."

"Mate." The word slipped off my tongue too easily.

Paris penciled it in. "It works. How did I miss that?" She glanced up at me. "How did *you* get that?"

I kept my gaze locked on the vase forming before me. Having a mate was common in the supernatural world, depending on the species. I was an oread, a mountain nymph, and while we didn't mate or bond, I knew enough supes who did. As for Paris, she was completely oblivious to Havenwood Falls' supernatural side. If she suspected something was off, she never mentioned it.

There was a rumble down the street, the sound of revving motorcycles getting louder as a group of men in leather vests cruised past our shop window.

Paris set her book aside and hugged her knees. "Do you think they're dangerous?"

I was too close to finishing the vase to look away. "SIN? No doubt."

SIN, or Swords of the Infernal Night, was Havenwood Falls' local motorcycle club. The club kept to itself, which was why it was rarely a topic of conversation in town. It was no secret they existed. They owned a delivery company, Cerberus Delivery Inc., and their trucks were the main means of delivering goods from outside town to businesses and individuals in Havenwood Falls. The sister of the club's vice president also owned Silk, an exclusive nightclub. But no one discussed them or their businesses, especially Silk's private clientele. I knew more than I should, because my father tended to talk too much about work at home. Not only did Cerberus—more commonly referred to as CDI—deliver unique goods to my father's business, but many of Silk's well-off clients liked buying expensive jewelry.

What *was* a secret—to the mortals anyhow—was that the leader of SIN, Liam Peters, and his business partner, Savage, were shapeshifting hellhounds. Most of their club members were supernatural. Maybe even all of them.

"The dangerous part is kind of hot," Paris admitted. "Though I wouldn't want to find out how dangerous," she rushed to add. "It's like wanting to eat an entire plate of chocolate. Tempting, but no."

Paris was diabetic, which played into her reserved nature. Her mother was overly protective, and Paris wasn't fond of testing her blood sugar or giving herself insulin shots in front of people.

"Why, Paris, are you into bad boys?" I teased.

She snorted. "As long as they're more 'rebel without a cause' and not Hannibal Lecter."

Finishing the vase, I glanced at her. "So, you'll warm the bed of a heartbreaker with a rap sheet, but not a serial killer. Noted."

Neither one of us had warmed anyone's bed. We were both going into our senior year at Havenwood Falls High in the fall, and neither of us had even been kissed. Paris was too shy, and I was always friend-zoned.

The studio door opened, and my sister, Leda, walked in, her brows arched. Pulling her key out of the lock, she shook it at us. "Why bolt the door when you have the closed sign up?"

The door being locked wasn't a bad thing, but it annoyed Leda when she had to dig for her keys instead of being able to just walk in.

"We're keeping rapscallions out." I gestured at her. "Case in point."

"Rapscallions?" Leda laughed, her gaze passing between us. "You two say the weirdest things. That word is seventeenth-century old."

"Tell that to Dad."

"Yeah, well, Dad's . . ." Her sentence trailed off, but I knew what she left unsaid. Dad's age predated the word. At six hundred ten years old, he predated a lot of things. "Can you catch the shipment for Apex out back and put out new inventory before we open on Monday?"

"Wasn't that supposed to come in yesterday?" Standing, I rushed to a paint-stained, industrial-sized sink built into the wall at the back of the room. The clay on my hands turned the water tan as it circled the basin to disappear down the drain.

I was a study in disarray, my unruly red hair bunched on top of my head, my body hidden by a light blue button-up shirt, overalls, and an apron. I was the complete opposite of my sister. She was tall where I was short, slender where I was skinny, blonde where I was redheaded, and elegant where I was laidback and disorganized.

Leda's heels clicked on the concrete floor, her red shoes complementing her black dress pants, black suit jacket, and red blouse. Her fingers sparkled. Rings were an everyday fashion accessory for her, and she had easy access to them. Not only did my family own the art studio on Main, but we also owned a jewelry store, Summit Jewelry, on the corner of Eighth and Main, next door. Like my sister and I, the two stores couldn't be any more different. While Apex was a chaotic, colorful shop that smelled like paint, Summit Jewelry was an elegant store with shining hardwood flooring, hanging chandeliers, and a showcase floor full of glass cases.

"Dad got word of a rare jewel he wanted at an auction outside town. He won the bid on it, and CDI was kind enough to wait the extra day to deliver. For an added fee, of course. I've already got the shipment for the jewelry store and locked up Dad's new prize. The jewel is pretty, I'll give him that, but it probably cost us a fortune." Bitter humor colored Leda's voice. "I'm headed back to the store. Make sure they don't break anything."

Tucking my hands into the pockets of my apron, I turned to Paris. "Want to help?"

"SIN is out back? As in now?" Her eyes went wide. Paris worked part time at Apex, but her hours rarely coincided with shipments.

"It *is* their delivery company."

She launched to her feet, instantly towering over me, and touched her hair nervously.

Leading the way, I opened a door at the back of the studio and stepped into a storeroom. Another door led into the alley, and it stood open, no doubt courtesy of my sister.

A boy I instantly recognized but had never met ducked into the space, wheeling a stack of boxes in front of him. He was tall, at least six feet two, and while that was intimidating, it was nothing compared to most hellhounds. He had a lot of room to grow. The white short-sleeve T-shirt stretched across his torso was mostly hidden by a plain leather cut, which meant he wasn't a part of the motorcycle club, but —if the rumors I'd heard were any indication—he also wasn't opposed to it. He was ripped, his muscles straining against the fabric as he unloaded the boxes. A thick chain tattoo wrapped his left arm, starting somewhere beneath his sleeve and circling down to his forearm. Other tattoos I couldn't make out peeked at us from under his right sleeve. Dark hair, cut close to his head but left longer on the top, fell carelessly onto his forehead, bringing attention to the expensive sunglasses covering his eyes.

Paris inhaled sharply behind me, trying desperately to make herself as small as possible, even though I made a terrible shield.

Jack Peters. Middle son of SIN's leader, Liam Peters. Although I didn't *know* him, I recognized him easily. He was seventeen and a rising senior at the prestigious Sun and Moon Academy, and we had a lot of the same acquaintances. I'd say friends, but I wasn't sure he had those. He was as elusive as his father and his father's club.

"Hi," I greeted him cheerfully. Jack didn't respond. I wasn't even sure he looked at me.

"You need help moving this stuff into the store?" a deep, raspy voice asked, and I nearly jumped out of my skin. Paris squeaked.

Purchase *Curse the Night* where books are sold.